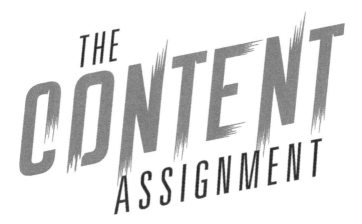

THE CONTENT ASSIGNMENT

HOLLY ROTH

DOVER PUBLICATIONS, INC.
Mineola, New York

Bibliographical Note

This Dover edition, first published in 2019, is an unabridged republication of the work published by Penguin Books Ltd., Harmondsworth, Middlesex, UK, in 1958.

Library of Congress Cataloging-in-Publication Data

Names: Roth, Holly, author.
Title: The content assignment / Holly Roth.
Description: Mineola, New York : Dover Publications, Inc., 2019. |
  "This Dover edition, first published in 2019, is an unabridged republication
  of the work published by Penguin Books Ltd., Harmondsworth,
  Middlesex, UK, in 1958."
Identifiers: LCCN 2018042499| ISBN 9780486832968 | ISBN 0486832961
Subjects: LCSH: Detective and mystery stories.
Classification: LCC PS3568.O85413 C66 2019 | DDC 813/.54—dc23
LC record available at https://lccn.loc.gov/2018042499

Manufactured in the United States by LSC Communications
83296101   2019
www.doverpublications.com

To my Mother

1

The minute I saw those few words at the bottom of one of the long columns in the previous Friday's *Times* I had the answer to the question of what I would do with my life. I had had the answer for two years, of course, but until that hot July morning I hadn't been able to do anything about it.

The item was at the tail end of a long description of the departure of the *Queen Elizabeth*. The fact that I was reading column after column of *The Times'* exhaustive detail shows the extent of my boredom with life. Morning after morning I sat in my small flat and read *The Times* like a proof-reader, comma by comma. If I got behind, as I currently had, I rushed furiously through the long, grey, out-dated columns, impelled, as I dimly knew, by the simple need to fill my life, to seem busy. I was doing free-lance writing, and very successfully, and I think my subconscious defence for the vast waste of time I permitted myself before settling down to work was that I might get a usable idea out of the news. Well, I got one that morning—usable in many senses.

My first impulse was to take off—just take off for America without further to-do. But common sense and financial considerations—the latter being so unavoidable in England these days—held me back. Free-lance writing doesn't pay when you aren't doing it—most things don't—but free-lancing is even more dependent upon output than most jobs. And other than the cheques I get for my articles, all I have is a few pieces of furniture, a portable typewriter, and £200 a year from my mother's estate.

So I called Nigel Lamson. I was put through quickly—I demanded to be put through quickly—and when I got him on the line I asked if I could come round and see him immediately. He mentioned that he had appointments, and I mentioned that he and I would never speak again, and I would never write a line for his paper again, if I didn't see him before lunchtime. Nigel knows me very well, and he had never heard me take such a tone before. So, more as a friend than as an editor, I suppose, he said, Oh, well—if it was like that.

I dressed, leaped into a cab, and was in Fleet Street fifteen minutes later.

Lamson is a very nice chap. He welcomed me into his cubbyhole of an office and gave me a cigarette and time to settle down before he said, "Now, John, what's it all about?"

I extracted the scrap I had torn off the bottom of Page 4 of the previous Friday's *Times*. "I've been reading the competition again—"

"Not competition. A way of life."

"—and in their usual extensive report of the sailing of the *Queen Elizabeth* I came across this item." I pointed. "Here."

Lamson took the snip of paper from me and read it carefully. He looked at me, and then he turned the paper over.

I said, "No. You had the right side in the first place. Read the part that starts, 'Among the other passengers . . .'"

He read it again. Then he cocked an eyebrow, and read the few words aloud: " 'Among the other passengers is Miss Ellen Content of New York who, after a brief stay in England, is returning to America to fill a series of dancing engagements.' Is that it?"

"That's it."

"I'm afraid, John, I'm no clearer."

"I want you to send me to New York on assignment. The assignment is to follow Miss Content's tour and then write a series of articles on it."

Nigel's eyebrows went up almost into his hairline. He stared at me for a minute, and then he said, "I take it you're serious?"

I leaned forward in my chair. "Nigel, listen to me. I'm deadly serious. I don't know what I'll get in the way of a story. I don't even know if I'll *get* a story. I've got to go for entirely personal reasons.

If you don't send me I'll manage on my own some other way. But if you do send me you stand a chance of getting a wonderful story. And if no story materializes I'll do a series for you—without payment—on any topic you name. I can only ask you to trust my instincts."

I sat back. "I suppose," I added slowly, "that's a lot of trust."

Nigel looked contemplatively at me and silence settled over the little room. It occurred to me that we looked very much alike. We're distinctly, and yet nondescriptly, British. We're both quite a bit over six feet tall, fairish, with a good deal of hair that we keep cropped very close, and regular features that don't seem outstanding in any particular way. Nigel is about forty-five, and so has ten years on me, and it is always comforting, when I look at him, to realize that if the parallel of our appearances holds up, I'm going to get older gracefully and almost imperceptibly.

He finally said, "What you're really asking, then, is that I, or rather, this paper, advance you money—lend you money—in an indeterminate amount, probably between five hundred and a thousand pounds—and battle the Bank of England for permission to allow that money to go out of the country."

"I suppose, if we must get down to unvarnished nutshells, that's about it. But I'm also giving you, as the paper's editorial head, a gambler's chance at what may be a very good story. Exclusive."

"And since you haven't yet offered me a hint of what this story is about, I expect you don't intend to?"

"No, I don't. I can't. It might be dangerous to the lives of the people involved."

Nigel looked startled. It was a dramatic comment. And Nigel and I, who are alike in more ways than appearance, don't often make, or even hear, dramatic pronouncements. We were both in the war, thoroughly in it, as a matter of fact, and we both did—well, creditably—but basically we are quiet men, conventional men. We're not the stuff of which dangerous living is made. And the quietness and conventionality I saw in Nigel's startled face was, I knew, reflected in mine.

Lamson said abruptly, "All right, John. You've been a good reporter—always delivered for me. Not all reporters have. I'll give you the—uh—assignment on the grounds that you've got a failure coming to you. Now, when do you want to leave?"

"I want to beat the *Elizabeth* to New York."

The eyebrows went up. "Then you'll have to fly. And fast. I'm pretty certain she docks in the States tomorrow morning—Tuesday."

He pushed a button on his desk. As his secretary entered the room he said, "Mrs. Brighton, please find out what planes are leaving for New York this afternoon or evening. Book passage for Mr. Terrant on the first available plane after"—he looked questioningly at me—"five o'clock?" I nodded—"five o'clock. Cable the New York office to have someone at the airport to advance expenses to Mr. Terrant. Then start an application to the Bank of England for permission to underwrite his expenses. File our request under 'The Content Assignment.' Also. . ."

2

At six that evening I took off from London Airport. At a quarter to five the next morning we landed, in sluicing rain, at Gander, Newfoundland. And there the big plane squatted, like a marooned and disconsolate duck. There was, we were given to understand, bad weather ahead also.

I almost went out of my mind in Gander. We were held up there for over an hour and a half. As I prowled the lounge and peered through the glass wall at the instruments that measured our impotency, I was filled with the formless fury that only elements can provoke—a rage that can find no satisfactory target. After nearly two years of waiting and seeking, I was within hours of Ellen Content, and there I had to sit. And while I sat and raged at the delay, my mind went into its well-worn groove, over and over the finding and losing of Ellen Content, seeking the answers with so pitifully few facts as a base for speculation.

It was raining the night I met Ellen, too. A nasty, cold drizzle was falling over Berlin, and I was talking with Ed Bigeby, an American newspaperman, in the lobby of a small hotel a few blocks behind the Adlon. We were both living in the second-rate little hotel, which had become a newspaperman's haven.

It was early autumn of 1948. I was a full-time working reporter on assignment in Berlin. I had seen service for four years in the infantry and had received a medical discharge—four bullets in my left leg had left me with a limp, which was getting rapidly less noticeable and less bothersome. I was thirty-two years old, and a fairly contented, happy man. My service in the Army was a blessedly faint memory. I had come out of it alive, and, compared to many, healthy. I was doing the work I liked best, and I was fortunate enough to be doing it in a city that was, at that moment, the news spot of the world.

Berlin, or what was left of it, was a busy, bustling place. Confusion reigned, and Babel was a small village with two visiting foreigners compared to the mess of languages in Berlin. The city had adjusted to the difficult business of absorbing the evacuees who were still pouring back in. De-nazification was almost completed in the British and American zones, proceeding slowly in the French zone, and almost not at all in the Russian sector.

The Russians' lack of good will or good faith was out in the open; they had walked out of the Allied Control Council that spring, begun the blockade, and announced that they would no longer participate in the four-power Kommandatura. The magnificent Allied air lift, raised to break the blockade, had been started, and it was going full tilt by the time I got there.

I had been in Berlin only two weeks, and I had been delighted to find Ed, whom I had known slightly before the war when he was working in the London office of the New York *Herald Tribune* and I was a rank beginner. At that time he had been kind and very helpful—without condescension—and he had certainly done far more to teach me my business than any of the people on my paper—more, for that matter, than any of my compatriots.

Bigeby was a large, bluff, laughing man who always knew the latest jokes. When he had brought you up to the moment on the new ones, he told you old ones—and their age or your familiarity with them didn't matter a bit, for he told them magnificently and there was more pleasure in the run of the story than in its point—a rare talent. There was something about his garrulity, his shining, good-natured face, his inability to remain still for more than a few seconds at a time, that caused many people to underestimate him. I was not one of those people. Ed Bigeby was not a fool; in addition to being a well-found companion, he was an experienced, intelligent newspaperman.

On that rainy night in Berlin, Bigeby was telling me a non-stop joke when he interrupted himself and called to a girl who was just going out of the door, "Hey, Ellen. Ellen!" The girl turned, smiled, and came towards us.

That moment will go on in my memory if I live for ever. And that makes excellent sense, because there are very few important moments in a lifetime. To see coming towards you the face that will mean an end of oneness is—far more than birth itself—the beginning of life. I suppose appearances don't mean very much and, in theory, a glimpse of her face could have been misleading—she could have been a silly girl or a stupid one. And yet that wasn't really possible because it was the intelligence, the shyness, and the warmness I saw in her face that mattered to me from that moment on.

Ellen was not conventionally pretty. Her face was too broad at the forehead and too narrow at the chin. And the breadth of its upper half was the more noticeable because of her black, arched brows. Her hair and eyes were so dark as to seem almost black, and, by contrast, her fair skin was startling. She had a small, rather indeterminate nose and a full but small mouth. She was a small girl altogether, and slight, and that day she was, unlike most American girls I'd met, almost shabbily dressed. She had on a brown mackintosh, and a very blue scarf—which I imagine she intended to bind over her head against the rain—fell loosely over her shoulders. Her beautiful hair, straight and soft and short, cut in a Dutch bob like a small English boy's, framed her small, pale face like a black mist.

As she came towards us I thought she looked defenseless, poignantly alone, but the impression receded when she spoke. Her low voice carried charm and intelligence and self-reliance, and the American drawl, which I always find pleasant, was, as it came softly from her lips, particularly musical.

She said, "Hello, Ed. Haven't seen you in a long time. Why aren't you out slaving for a living?"

"Nothing ever happens in this flea-hole of a town. But you—what are *you* doing in our den of iniquity? Don't tell me you've deserted that girls'-club kind of joint you live in that I can never seem to pry you out of?"

She smiled—shyly, but with a kind of inward assurance. "I'm using your lobby as an alley, walking one block—from the north door to the south door—inside. The heavens have just opened and it's darn damp outside. Why a den of iniquity? Just because it's full of newspapermen?"

"Isn't that enough? And here's another newspaperman for you. This is Johnny Terrant. He's on an English paper, so you might take a chance and come eat some dinner with us. English newspapermen are *gentlemen*. This is Ellen Content, Johnny."

I took her small hand and said, "Nobody in the whole world—except Ed—calls me Johnny. Will you call me John, and join us for a bit of dinner?"

She said, "Yes, John. I'd like that."

3

FOR an evening so memorable, I must admit that nothing very memorable occurred. We went to the Adlon, much to Ed's surprise. But I felt inexplicably expansive, and insisted upon doing it with flourishes. Over dinner I asked her what she was doing in Berlin, and she said, "I'm a civilian typist attached to the Army's office of information—over on Unter den Linden. The American Army, of course."

I remember that I was surprised. Those comprehending eyes, that high forehead, only partially obscured by the black bang, and her understanding of the political situation didn't seem at all compatible with a typist's job.

I asked her, "And what did you do before—was it patriotism? a desire to see the world?—brought you here?"

She laughed. She had a charming laugh, a really gay laugh that took all the sadness out of her eyes. "I'm afraid it was nothing more important than a desire to see the world," she said. "I was a schoolteacher in New York City. A very minor one, teaching the lower grades in the public grammar schools. History and geography."

That seemed more like it. She would be a good teacher, I thought. Sympathetic, understanding, warm. It was easy to visualize her in front of her class—loved and loving.

The only odd incident of the evening occurred as we discussed dessert. Although Ellen and I considered the prospect with horror, Ed wanted dessert, and he wouldn't give in and order the inevitable strudel. He insisted on his right to choose from the elaborate list on the menu, but he couldn't catch the headwaiter's eye to get one of the enormous menus from which we had ordered the first part of our dinner. Then Ellen said, in a rather vague way, "Dessert? Well, now, let me see. There's a choice of—" and she rattled off twenty or so fancy dessert descriptions in the part French, part language-of-the country that is so typical of menus in expensive restaurants the world over.

When she had finished her recitation there was a moment of startled silence, and then Ed said, "Don't tell me! Let me guess. You're leading a double life. In the evenings you're having an affair with the chef. Better yet, you're an international spy and this is headquarters, the meeting place for the members of Local Fifty-two, International Organization GT 8. You're been here so often you know the menu by heart and when you are—"

I interrupted. "*Do* tell me. I can't guess. Have you been here so often?"

Ellen shook her head shyly. She had flushed a little and the soft colour was charming against her hair. "I've been here only once before. It's—it's the result of two little tricks—a knack for languages, and the ability of total recall."

Good memories have always fascinated me. I'm a forgetter by nature. I asked, "Do you remember by seeing? That is, are you one of those people who can recall anything once you've seen it written down?"

She said, "No, the trick doesn't seem to be limited. What I've seen, heard, overheard"—she laughed a little—"anything. I can reproduce a map, for instance, although I have little drawing ability, and on the other hand, I can sing an odd tune I've heard only once—though I certainly have no voice. It's the direct reason for my language facility, of course. And it also accounts for my teaching history and geography. No brains, you see, just simple facts."

Ed said, "What a heaven-sent opportunity! Johnny, tell you what: we'll go into a three-way partnership as blackmailers. Ellen can walk through the corridors upstairs at night, listening, and then without an incriminating word on paper we'll—"

I said, "And the language facility accounts for your job with the Army, despite your youth."

The black mist swayed softly as she shook her head. "I'm twenty-five years old, John. Some of the typists at the office are considerable younger than that."

Of course. She had been a schoolteacher. She couldn't very well be the nineteen-year-old she looked to me. I had got the impression because of the shyness of her, the quietness, the complete repose. Young girls, after the early tom-boy teens and before the competitive, jangling twenties, sometimes go through an unselfconscious, restful stage during which they achieve a transient composure. That was what had misled me in Ellen—the peace of her.

I saw Ellen Content twice more before the last time. Just four times altogether. We were together three evenings and one afternoon, in a period of a week, and on those four meetings I'd built my life ever since.

The next night I took her dancing—a light mist moving quietly in my arms. And on that Sunday afternoon we went walking, saying little, I suppose, although we seemed to learn a great deal about each other. All the things we learned we had in common. We were both without relatives, for instance. That's a stranger fact than you might think—but we were each the only child of now-deceased only-children parents, and we didn't have the uncles, aunts, and cousins most people seem to have dotted around.

We walked in the beautiful Tiergarten, and in spite of the war's damage and the wet early-autumn weather, it was a lovely walk. Once as we sauntered along, following the winding lanes and lakes, a child's ball hit me and cannoned off into the thick underbrush. I went after it and tossed it to the youngster. As I started back across the fifteen feet of grass separating me from Ellen I saw again, as I had each time we approached each other, the defenseless look, the aloneness of her. But when I reached her it was gone, and it was then, I think, that I knew finally. With me, she was shy but laughing. And the gay laugh chased the aloneness, and it was a rout that only I could perform.

That was the day she told me something about myself. "I think you're rather like me, John," she said as we sat on a bench watching the play of sun and shadow on the little lake before us. "People think we're self-sufficient, reserved, perhaps even taciturn, but we're really just shy. In you, at least, the quality masquerades as 'British reserve'—but in me it's more noticeable because it's so unlike most Americans."

And she said, "It's odd that we should be so much alike and look so different. You're tall and I'm small. And you're fair and I'm dark, and your skin is tanned till it's really very brown, and mine is stubbornly light."

"So we will always be able to let people satisfy their urge for the old clichés by telling themselves that opposites attract. But we'll know better."

"Yes," she said.

And there it was, as simply as that. Our always was taken care of.

4

ELLEN said she had some work to clear up that Sunday night, but she agreed to join me on Monday evening for dinner.

When I got back to my hotel room late on Monday afternoon, the phone was ringing. It was Ellen, and it seemed to me that she sounded rather upset.

"I'm glad I reached you, John. Do you mind if Ed Bigeby and a girl join us this evening?"

"Well, I'd rather be alone with you. But if he wants to, and you don't mind—"

"He didn't especially want to. I'm afraid I rather insisted."

"I see." I didn't.

"I feel—responsible. He dropped by the office and stopped to say hello. Natasha—her name is Natasha Paviloff—was sitting beside my desk—and you know Ed. He immediately insisted on taking her out. So I feel responsible."

"She's very young?"

"She's twenty-three."

"I see," I said again. But it didn't seem to me quite necessary for a twenty-five-year-old to protect a twenty-three-year-old. And Ed's wolf-like exterior was just that—a surface thing. After ten minutes with him anyone could see that he was certainly not a threat. But whatever Ellen wanted was all right with me, and so from a real desire to help her out, I said, "These European girls are brought up in such a protected way sometimes—"

Ellen said flatly, "She's an exotic dancer."

There was a pause. Then I said, "Ellen, in some ridiculous way I seem to have put you on the defensive. Whatever you want is just fine with me."

"Thank you, John. I can't explain—exactly. Collect Ed and pick us up at my *pension,* yes?"

"We'll be there."

We were at the big boarding-house at a quarter to seven. Ed was bubbling over, and when Ellen came down the stairs into the common-room and introduced me to Natasha I could see the reason for his exuberance. Natasha was a tall blonde with long hair and long bones. Her movements were feline, graceful. She was, as Ed had told me several times on the way over, "a dish."

She also seemed to be a nice girl. After a very few minutes in her company, the exotic cheekbones, green eyes, long swaying hair, and romantic accent were replaced in my impressions by her basic wholesomeness.

When the four of us got into the street I found myself at a loss for a suggestion where to go. I hadn't thought beyond the moment of seeing Ellen—but when I was faced with the need to decide on food and entertainment, I found it was not an easy decision. We were an ill-assorted quartet—the ebullient Bigeby, the quiet Ellen, the exotic Natasha, and my own rather stiff self.

We stood on the pavement for a minute while I struggled for a thought, but Bigeby beat me to it. "Let's all go to The Russian Inn," he said heartily. "Can't think of a better place. I know a way to get over there that isn't a bit dangerous—"

Natasha said flatly, "No."

Ed looked surprised and a little chagrined, and Ellen spoke up quickly. I had a feeling she was rushing in to smooth things over, but I didn't know what things or why they needed smoothing. She said, "Well, Ed, I don't think it's a very good idea. It would be a sort of busman's holiday for Natasha—"

Natasha said firmly, "And eet ees impossible." There was an insurmountable finality in her voice.

That finality definitely needed smoothing over. I said, "It's still quite early. Let's have a drink before we decide on dinner."

I thought a little of that common denominator might help bring us to a mutual decision.

We were fairly near Ed's and my hotel, so we wandered back there and settled in a small, dim, deserted lounge just off the lobby. But before we could order a drink I was paged. The boy said I was wanted on the phone, so I went to the telephones near the main desk, asked for my call, and said, "Hello?"

The male voice that instantly poured out of the receiver was so excited and uneven that I couldn't get a word of what he was saying. I realized after a moment that more than his excitement was standing in the way of my understanding; he wasn't speaking either English or German. I couldn't place the language at all.

Then I caught two constantly repeated words—"Content" and "Natasha."

I said, "Hold on, please," left the receiver dangling, and went back to the little lounge.

"Ellen," I said, "it seems to be for you. Or Natasha. I can't understand the language."

Natasha rose straight up out of her low chair as if someone had jerked a string. I don't think I had ever seen terror so clearly expressed on a face before.

Ellen sat in complete composure for perhaps ten seconds. Then she said sharply, "Sit down, Natasha!" Natasha sat down again as if someone had dropped the string. Ellen said to me, "Please take me to the telephone, John."

We marched back across the lobby. I remember thinking, *en route,* that I would not have believed it possible for so small a girl to move so quickly without running, and without giving too great an impression of speed.

At the desk Ellen grabbed the dangling phone and said, "Hello?"—but the rest of her conversation was incomprehensible to me. I realized in the middle of the short phrases she was very nearly barking into the mouthpiece that the language was probably Russian.

After a full minute of the gibberish she hung up and stood motionless, staring at the wall. Then she turned around and transferred the blank stare to me.

I said urgently, "Ellen!"

She answered, "Yes, John. Let's go back to the table." But her preoccupation had not been broken.

As we moved back across the lobby she said over her shoulder, "You'll help if I need you, John?"

"Of course. At any time, in any way."

She smiled up at me and said, "Thank you." But I still had the bewildered feeling that I was on the periphery of her attention, that something had taken her far away from me.

When we reached the table, Ellen sat down without speaking and took a small notebook and a pencil out of her bag. She tore out a sheet of blank paper and wrote something on it.

Natasha looked as if she hadn't moved since we left the table, and Ed looked bewildered. Natasha opened her mouth, as if it were a difficult gesture to accomplish, and asked, "Papa?"

Ellen was very brisk. It struck me that she even *looked* brisk. The cloudy black hair was still cloudy, but it was I thought insanely, a *disciplined* cloud. The beautiful dark eyes seemed to have gained depth and purpose. Her always erect carriage, which had previously seemed charming and endearing in one so small, now looked forceful and determined. When she spoke there was a timbre in her still melodious voice that I had not heard there before.

She said to Natasha, "Yes, it was Papa. But nothing has really happened. Now, please do exactly as I ask. Ed"—Ed switched his puzzled gaze from Natasha to Ellen—"Ed, take Natasha to this address." She handed him the slip of paper on which she had made a note, "When you get there, ring the door-bell four times—little, short rings. When the door opens, say, 'I've come about the bathroom pipe.' They'll let Natasha in. Then destroy this address, go and have a drink and some dinner, and forget the whole thing.

"Ed"—she leaned forward and her voice took on a persuasive ring, a note of real strength—"it's not easy to dismiss such an adventure. Especially if you're a newspaperman. But lives, many lives, including Natasha's, hang on your behaviour. And if you got a story no one would let you print it. So forget it. Don't go into the house, and don't hang around after you've delivered Natasha.

"Natasha, go with Ed. Wait there. I'll come soon. And I'll bring them with me."

Ellen turned and looked at me. It was an odd feeling to have her look at me like that. This time her defenselessness was gone not because I was present but because she was caught up in another world in which she didn't really need me at all. But after a second she took me with her into that world because she said, "Do you want to come with me, John?"

5

IN front of the hotel we hailed two cabs. Natasha and Ed got into the first. I noticed that Ed was almost carrying Natasha, who still behaved like a marionette whose strings were slack. Ellen and I got into the second taxi, and she called out a rather lengthy address in German. I've wondered since if she was deliberately protecting me from that address by making it sound as complicated as possible.

We skidded along the wet streets of Berlin for what seemed like a considerable length of time until we were in a remote suburban section. The houses were pleasant, comfortably middle-class, rather like Maida Vale in London. We stopped in front of one of them, got out, and I paid and dismissed the driver. We had started up the walk to the front door when Ellen stopped. She stood perfectly still on the dark walk, staring at the front door, which was clearly visible in the soft light from within. I followed her gaze and realized why, in the dark night, the entrance was so evident. The door was partially open.

Then Ellen started to run.

We entered into a hall. It was a big house, and in addition to the stairway going upward there was a bewildering multiplicity of doors. But Ellen had apparently been there before. She went directly to the door on the left of the entrance and opened it. Then we were in a drawing-room, an empty drawing-room. We stood still for a minute and then we heard a soft rustle from a farther door at the rear of the drawing-room. Ellen rushed towards that rear door, and I kept pace behind her.

We entered an old-fashioned, overfurnished back parlour. On the floor was an elderly man, his face almost obscured by a magnificent beard. He was bleeding profusely from a wound in his stomach. A telephone receiver was lying beside him and the body of the instrument was a foot away. But the fact that the receiver was off made no difference because, farther along, the wire had been cut, and it was hanging uselessly about three feet from the box on the wall. On the opposite side of the room a handsome woman of late middle age was sitting on the floor, her back against a chair's legs. Her hair was meticulously groomed into a pile on top of her head. For a moment I didn't understand why she didn't get up and help the old man. Then I noticed her foot. It was sticking out at an odd angle.

She said, in a strained whisper in fairly good English, "They didn't know he had called. He tricked them. We saw them outside, and he quickly telephoned you. Then as they came in he pretended he was just starting to try to get a call through—and he quickly dropped the receiver as if they had caught him. He hoped he would gain a reprieve—but they shot him anyway."

Tears started to fall down her cheeks, but her expression of supreme shock didn't change and her whisper remained even and clear. It occurred to me that she was so deep in a nightmare that she had lost reality. She spoke as if from a dream world, her gaze set, and her facial muscles unmoving, despite the tears. "Then one of them went upstairs to look for Natasha. When they couldn't find her, they said they were going out to pick her up, and they would be back. One of them stamped on my leg"—she didn't look down—"so I wouldn't be able to go for help. Have you got Natasha, Miss Content? You promised, Miss Content."

Ellen still stood just in front of me, where she had arrested her pell-mell flight into the room. She said, "I've got her, Mrs. Paviloff. I've got her safe as I promised I would have, under the name we all agreed on. She's waiting for you. And now I'll take you to her. Has he told you anything, Mrs. Paviloff?"

"No. He never will. He says Natasha and I must be safe."

The bearded old man on the floor said something I couldn't understand. I realized, as I heard the accented word "Content" followed by a question mark, that he was the man who had called the hotel.

Ellen said, "Yes. I'm right here, Mr. Paviloff." Then, as she went to him, she branched into Russian again. She knelt beside the old man, and after a minute she sat down and took his head in her lap. He started to talk, a gasping, rasping, guttural series of tones—each sounding as if it were his last.

I said, "Ellen, shall I go for help?"

She looked up at me from the old man's face almost with irritation, as if I had interrupted an important business conference. Then her face cleared, and she said, "No, John. You heard her. They'll be back. So the important thing is to get her out of here."

"What about him? He's in worse condition, I should think."

"Too much worse, John. It would be pointless."

"Oh." I paused to assimilate the unaccustomed idea of death in the back parlour. Then I added, "Well, then, what about you? If they'll be back—whoever 'they' are—I certainly don't want you waiting here to greet them."

She shook her head impatiently. "Think for a minute, John. Mrs. Paviloff says they didn't know he had telephoned. So they have no reason to suspect that anyone will be here. If they return before I've left all I'll have to do is to go out of the back door, or hide in the coal-bin, or even under a bed. They're not going to search for someone they don't think is here."

"But they'll search for Mrs. Pav—*her*."

"Think, John. Think! Because they'll think. They'll think that if Mrs. Paviloff managed to walk, as she will seem to have done, she would walk *out*—to get help. So they'll be in more of a hurry than ever, because they'll decide that people are coming. No, John. I'll be all right. Just take her and get out of here as fast as possible." She started murmuring to the old man again.

I stood helplessly in the entrance-way to the room. I had been rooted to that spot since we came through the door. I said, "But, Ellen, her leg is broken. If I lift her without a proper splint the pain will be excruciating."

Ellen looked up at me impatiently, and then a small sweet smile broke through and for a minute I had the Ellen I loved back again. But it was a very small minute, because her next words were quite other than my short experience with her had taught me to expect. "John, dear. You knock her out with a short right to the chin. Or a left, whichever you are better at. To save her the pain. Then you lift her up and walk out of the door. You go a short block to the right, where you'll be on a more frequented street. You get the first cab, which won't be easy, because there won't be many in this neighbourhood at this hour. If necessary, hail a car and pray they speak some English—your German is not the most comprehensible I've heard. Tell them you had an automobile accident and your car won't operate. Get them to take you to the Unter den Linden office. When you get there ask for William Eider. He'll be there, even at this hour. Explain exactly what has happened here. Mr. Eider will take Mrs. Paviloff to join Natasha. And he'll get a doctor to her. Her leg will be no worse in half an hour than it is now. Then you go home and follow the instructions I gave Ed. I'll call you in the morning."

It was the most difficult assignment I'd ever been handed. But Ellen somehow made me feel that she would have done it—just like that. So, of course, I had to manage it. I approached Mrs. Paviloff warily, but she didn't seem to have heard a word and was therefore completely defenseless.

As I left the room carrying the unconscious Mrs. Paviloff, who, incidentally, was heavy, the sound of the old man's conversation and Ellen's answers followed me through the living-room. The old man would whisper a series of guttural phrases, and then Ellen would croon something that sounded very much the same. It sounded almost like a litany, and I found myself wondering if it could be the Russian Orthodox last rites.

The thought was foolish, of course, and I shrugged it off.

6

I DISLIKE thinking about the next half-hour. I carried out my instructions, and it all worked out exactly as Ellen had predicted it would.

By the time I had reached the corner one block to my right, my knees were buckling, and I was gasping for breath—and Mrs. Paviloff had gained weight. But I had the luck of getting a taxi immediately, and the driver did understand a little English. He understood just little enough, fortunately, because when he wanted to know why I didn't take my mother to a hospital my exhaustion and confusion had robbed me of ingenuity and I simply recited one of the Shakespeare sonnets very quickly over and over in a reasonable-sounding tone of voice.

At the Army office I propped Mrs. Paviloff up in a corner of the car and asked the driver to wait. Then I went up the walk and pressed the bell.

A young woman answered my steady pressure on the door-bell, and in response to my question, said, "Mr. Eider? One minute, please." She did not ask me to enter the building, and I stood chafing on the steps until the door was opened again.

This time a tall, heavy, shirt-sleeved man of about thirty-five stood silhouetted in the lighted opening. He said, "I'm William Eider. Yes?"

I said, "Ellen Content told me to come to you. I have a Mrs. Paviloff with me. She's out in the taxi." I waved at the kerb behind me. "You know the name—Paviloff? Ellen said you would. She—that is—Ellen said—"

Eider said, "Just a minute." The door closed again and I was left on the step with my mouth open, still seeking a starting point in the story.

Eider reappeared a second later, shrugging on a coat. He passed me and started down the steps. Over his shoulder he said to me, "Go on."

I rushed after him, groping through what seemed the pertinent facts, though I had little certainty of what was pertinent. I felt I had barely started when we reached the taxi.

He put his fingers on the door-handle and said, "All right, Mr. Uh—all right, I'll get the rest later. Now you go have a drink or go back to your place and go to bed. Forget what—"

"I know the rest of it," I said bitterly. "I've been thoroughly briefed by Ellen."

"Good. We'll be in touch with you."

He stepped into the taxi, and that was that.

I had no intention of going to my hotel for a drink. I was going back for Ellen. But there was a flaw in that plan. I had no idea of where she was. I had never found out the Paviloffs' address. So I looked instead for Ed. But I was stopped in that effort, too—he wasn't in his hotel room, he wasn't in his office, and he wasn't in either of the only two bars I had ever seen him frequent.

I spent the remainder of the night lying in my bed, but I didn't sleep.

At exactly nine o'clock the next morning I called the Unter den Linden place. I was told that Miss Content hadn't come in yet. I called her *pension*. I was told she wasn't in. I called the office back. I kept that up until noon. At noon, the Army operator said, "Oh, yes. You called before, didn't you?"

My "yes" was bitter.

"Well, will you hold on a minute, please?"

After several minutes a deep masculine voice said, "Who's calling Miss Content?"

"This is John Terrant."

"May I ask your business with Miss Content?"

"It's personal."

"Oh. Well, I'm afraid she's going to be unavailable for the next several days. This is William Eider, Miss Content's superior. If there's any way I can—"

"Mr. Eider, we met last night."

"We did?"

"At your door. I delivered—"

"A package?" he interrupted. "You brought it in a cab? It had been sent to me by Miss Content?"

"Yes, I suppose it could be put that way. If you want to be mysterious about it."

Mr. Eider's voice turned very sharp. "I certainly do want to be mysterious about it. I should think the experience, the—er—events, would have made it clear to you that there is an element of secrecy about the package."

"I'm sorry. I expect you are right. But, you see, I've had a very bad morning. I've been given a tossing around—what you Americans call a 'runaround.' And I'm extremely anxious to speak to Miss Content. Naturally."

"Mr.—Oh, your name is Terrant."

"*Yes!*"

"Yes. Well, Miss Content left a message for you. She has gone away temporarily, but she asked me to tell you that she will be in touch with you as soon as it is possible. You're a newspaperman, aren't you, Mr. Terrant?"

"Yes. On assignment here."

"I see." Mr. Eider's voice was sharp again. There was a little silence. Then he said briskly, "Well, I'm afraid that's all I can do for you. Good-bye."

I banged the receiver cradle for a few seconds, but he had rung off. Then I sat and stared at the dead instrument.

I was filled with a fury I don't think I had ever experienced before. I expect it was not an entirely unself-seeking kind of anger; a good deal of "they can't do this to me" was mixed in with my concern for Ellen. I stormed out of my hotel and over to the American office on the wide, placid-looking avenue.

When I had announced my intention of seeing Mr. Eider immediately to the girl at the desk in the lobby, she said, "Yes, Mr. Eider is expecting you. Will you come this way?"

William Eider was in a little room at the left front of the ugly old mansion. In its early days the room most probably had served as a reception corner in which visitors waited while the butler announced them. The small cubicle was panelled in dark oak, making it seem even smaller, and Eider and the massive desk behind which he was standing seemed to crowd it almost to capacity.

Eider looked tired. Or perhaps he always looked melancholy and worn—I had no previous acquaintanceship to use for comparison. But his face was drawn into deep lines that seemed out of place on a man so little older than myself, and his large form was sagging heavily from the rigidly held shoulders.

But despite the deep circles beneath his eyes, the eyes themselves were alert and understanding. He seemed to take all of me in at once and to digest the whole quickly and competently.

He said, "Will you close the door on your way out, Miss Blakely?" And to me, "Please sit down. You English aren't supposed to behave dramatically, but at the moment you are doing what is commonly referred to as 'towering over me.'"

I suppose I was. I sat down beside his big desk and opened my mouth. But that was as far as I got.

He said, "Please, Mr. Terrant. Light a cigarette or a pipe or whatever the devil will calm you and sit still for a few minutes. Then I'll tell you what I can."

He sat still himself, looking out on the sunlit square. The sun filtered through the linden trees outside and made a lacy pattern across his desk. He stared down at the flickering pattern and looked very, very weary.

He finally said, "Now, look. Ellen Content left for America this morning. She is, and I am, as you undoubtedly have figured out by now—if you ever take time out for thinking instead of acting—members of the CIA. You British are so self-contained— usually—that you can afford to call a spade a spade. When you say 'Intelligence' or 'Counter-intelligence' your inherent use of understatement makes the words sound as if you were describing a grocery store. We Americans, on the other hand, are so innately dramatic that we have to put up blocks against ourselves. So we try to disguise our dramatic tendencies behind dull titles. Until a couple of years ago it was the 'Office of Strategic Services.' Now it's the 'Central Intelligence Agency.'

"However, no matter what its title, the Central Intelligence Agency is a spy service and a dangerous one. It doesn't often break out into raw drama such as you saw last night, and when it does, it's because the drama was forced on us. And the whole situation becomes even more important. Do you understand?"

I nodded. I didn't understand, and I was in no mood for a dissertation on the relative national traits of the Americans and the British. But I appeared to be getting a few facts, so it seemed like a good plan to let him proceed.

"Well, that's all there is to it. Miss Content is now safely on her way to America on—business—and she will be in touch with you as soon as she finds it prudent to do so."

My fury broke out again. I had waited for facts, and I had got nothing. "That's not all there is to it! How could she get to America? I don't think there was a single way out of here—boat, plane, or through train—this morning. And what happened to the Paviloffs? And where is Ed Bigeby?"

Mr. Eider said wearily, "An Army plane flew Miss Content out for—part of the way. Mrs. Paviloff and Miss Paviloff are safe. Mr. Paviloff died. And—" He paused, and then said deliberately, "Mr. Edward Bigeby was killed in a street fight at eleven o'clock last night. If you had been attending to your business this morning you would undoubtedly have heard that shocking news. It seems, Mr. Terrant, that he loitered where he shouldn't have and probed where he shouldn't have. I really would suggest that you take your lesson from his experience."

It certainly had an effect on me. Outside of my great affection for Ed, there was the inescapable fact that I'd be no good to Ellen or myself if I were dead.

Into the silence, Mr. Eider dropped a few more words. "Mr. Paviloff knew your name. Natasha must have told him whom she and Ellen were going to spend the evening with, because when he phoned the *pension* and the landlady told him that his daughter and Miss Content had left there, he called your hotel, and luckily found you all there. So it is not impossible—although I think it's unlikely—that you may already be known to—them." He left the threat hanging there.

I said, "All right, Mr. Eider. I'm sufficiently impressed. I shall try to do whatever you say. But let's look at my side of it for a minute. I love Miss Content. It's as if my wife, or my child, were snatched from me. Would you, if you were I, do nothing, ask nothing, just sit with your hands folded?"

He considered the point before he answered, and when he spoke I felt that he was being honest with me and with himself. "The analogy of a child is unfair. One is entirely responsible for a child. But if it were my wife, and she had chosen to help her country in such a way—and before I'd met her, at that; before she owed me any allegiance—I would feel bound to mind my business and wait for her to get in touch with me when she found herself able to do so."

"All right, Mr. Eider." His tiredness had communicated itself to me. "Just one more question. Who are the Paviloffs?"

He looked surprised. "Didn't you know? I guess you've been in Berlin a very short time. Well, there's no secret about that. The Paviloffs ran a quite famous restaurant called, not too surprisingly, The Russian Inn. They weren't White Russians or anything dramatic. Just a couple of immigrants who wandered into Berlin twenty-five or so years ago and started operating a small restaurant. When the city was partitioned after the surrender, the Inn happened, by coincidence, to fall into the zone assigned to the Russians. That cut down the Western patronage considerably of late. But many of us on this side still managed to get over there.

"Paviloff did very well on the whole, and some years ago he turned the place into a small cabaret. Natasha danced there and attracted a good deal of attention. That's all. No political history; nothing interesting."

And that was the end of the interview. That was the end of everything.

7

ONE doesn't exist for thirty-two years untouched by the slightest impulse towards marriage, then find somebody one loves deeply and immediately—and dismiss her disappearance, whatever the purported reasons for it, with a shrug.

It simply isn't in the nature of man.

I felt sorry for Mr. Eider, I admired him for what was clearly dedication to his duty and his country, and I could even understand his attitude. But I couldn't live by it, or try to match it as a pattern for my behaviour.

I am not a detective, and I was, if possible, still less of one then, but even I could see that certain lines of inquiry were clearly indicated.

The next morning I telephoned my office and told the editor that, for urgent personal reasons, I needed to take a few days off. He sounded surprised, but he didn't make any objections. Then I went down to the hotel's desk.

The desk clerk and I went into our usual routine: I spoke in my wildly improbable German, and he replied in a truly atrocious English. After the badly enunciated good morning and *guten Tag,* I asked him where The Russian Inn was. He told me the names of the streets that bounded it and turned to his left to point them out on the map of Berlin pinned to the wall. But the map reminded him.

"In the sector of the Russia Government it is. This is not goot."

I lapsed into English. "But indicated. In fact, I should say inevitable."

I left him looking puzzled.

Things weren't quite as bad in Berlin in 1948 as they got to be a little later. At any rate, it was easily possible, though not advisable, to crash the Eastern sector.

I crashed it. As I tacked across the city—looking, I suppose, remarkably British—my biggest problem arose from my decision to avoid cabs. I felt that it would be tempting fate to get into any conversations, with taxi drivers or anyone else.

I walked many miles that day. I had equipped myself with a "Guide to Berlin," which contained diagrams of the streets and printed directions. But the directions turned out to be useless—the heavy Gothic script was completely beyond my comprehension—and the diagrams were little better because they had been drawn before the war. The "landmarks" were more often missing than not.

I suppose that, as I stood helplessly on corner after corner trying to work out my whereabouts, I was just as conspicuous as I would have been if I'd been asking questions.

Then when I did find The Russian Inn I almost fell into the place before I knew I had arrived. And that was not so good. Because what looked like an army of Russian soldiers, complete with gleaming bayonets, were patrolling the premises.

The Russian Inn had a surprisingly charming exterior. It looked not unlike a rather large, sprawling, South African colonial mansion, its coat of white paint clean and fresh. And hanging on the door, clearly visible from the pavement forty feet away, was the largest padlock I had ever seen.

I am not a very good actor. Besides, I had been taken by surprise. I hadn't expected to fall over the Inn at that bend in the street; I hadn't expected the soldiers to be there at all—to say nothing of the astounding number of them; and I hadn't expected the padlock. So instead of sauntering casually and innocently onward, I stopped dead in my tracks, stared openly, and then about-faced and got out of there. It was an obvious rout.

If those soldiers had been British, American, French—any of a dozen nationalities—the lack of subtlety in the manoeuvre would have been immediately noticed by them. But the Russians—? Well,

I dislike making generalizations, but in my experiences with them they have been unvaryingly stupid, or at least, unperceptive.

I was a full block away before I heard sounds of pursuit—sounds they never should have made because, after they had made me aware of their pursuit, all I had to do was step into the ruins of a large block of flats, mount to the second storey, and watch them through a hole which a kitchen sink—I think—had left behind when it went through the mortar. I could have dodged around inside that shell of a building and evaded them for hours and hours, but it didn't become necessary; they never so much as looked at the ruin.

In the early dusk I left the cold, damp pile of stones and traipsed back across Berlin. This time I did no zigzagging. I simply aimed at the setting sun and made for it as quickly as I could.

And there went my first lead.

In a way, however, my day hadn't been entirely wasted. The *affaire* Paviloff and the disappearance of Ellen took on a new dimension for me—the dimension of reality. There was something about that padlock and those soldiers that spelled out for me the importance, the international importance, of Ellen's job.

The next morning I awakened to the awareness of a series of dull aches. A gutted, and consequently windy, stone building is no place in which to spend a damp autumn day. I had, not a cold, but rather a series of colds—one in my shoulder, one in my still not completely healed left leg, and an assortment of other vagrant pains. But, nevertheless, I was up, dressed, had had breakfast, and was out in the street by nine o'clock. Because if the international importance of the business had been brought home to me by my experience at The Russian Inn, the life-and-death seriousness of it did not need to be rammed home. Ed's death had made that crystal clear.

So, as my next step, I went around to Ed's paper's office. I knew the branch editor, Nick Holland, only slightly, but he was glad to see me; expatriates are always drawn together. Besides, on that day he seemed lonely. I sat beside his magnificently untidy desk; he slid down in his swivel chair and put his feet up on top of the great tangle of papers; and we talked.

As we talked, I began to realize how very fond of Ed he had been. I don't know why I was surprised; after all, I, too, had been fond of Ed. I think, in retrospect, that although Ed was one of those people whom everybody loves, each friend thought he stood alone in his affection, that he alone realized the worth and depth behind a seemingly shallow, good-natured exterior.

Finally, and none too tactfully, I put the thought into words: said I hadn't realized how fond of Ed Bigeby Holland had been.

"Why shouldn't I have been?" Holland stared belligerently at me. "He was a nice guy, and I worked with him for over twelve years, in three countries."

"I didn't know that."

"Tell you something else no one ever seemed to know." Holland seemed defensive. "He was a hell of a good newspaperman. He would have had my desk except that he was too hot on his feet—we couldn't spare him. Perhaps the fact that he so often seemed like a blundering idiot helped him, but whatever the reason he got more beats and more inside information than any six other guys I've ever known."

"A surprisingly keen chap," I agreed. "Too bad he had to die so pointlessly."

Holland examined his shineless shoes.

I decided to tackle it, and I used his silence as a starting place. "Or *did* he?" I added.

Holland took his eyes off the shoes and fastened them on me. "Under your hat?" he asked.

"Under—? Oh! Oh, yes. Definitely."

"Well, I'm not permitted to print a word of it. Not even supposed to let out a peep about it. Don't know why I am telling you. Except—Hell, I guess I do know why." He looked strangely embarrassed and furiously angry.

"The truth would be a kind of epitaph," he said. "Everyone would know he had been working, doing something worth while, not—brawling in the streets. But my government has forbidden me to—Another American died the next night. They said he was run over by a truck, and they buried him under a fake name. I was throttled that time, too. Something is up, you see? And Ed, as usual, had a toe in it."

"How do you know? Maybe——"

His feet came down with a crash and he flung his words at me. "I know because he *told* me! He called me at ten o'clock Sunday night. Told me to hold the night cable and get out the old code books. I asked him what he had, but he said he wasn't sure yet himself." He sat back in his chair and looked dispirited.

I was embarrassed. I felt as I were dealing off the bottom of the pack. I said lamely, "Too bad."

"It's the man, not the story," he added broodingly. "And I'd sure like his friends back home to know the truth. This way he is made to seem such a——a no-good."

When I left, his feet were back on the desk, and he was again staring moodily at his shoes.

I had had three leads: The Russian Inn, Ed's death, Ellen's *pension.* The third netted me no more than the first two.

I called myself Mr. Smythe—and I was very glad I had taken that precaution, because Mrs. Hoffer, who ran the *pension,* which Ed had so aptly called "a girls'-club kind of joint," was the distillation of all landladies the world over. She knew nothing, but she was willing—eager—to gossip. In spite of a wealth of detail and many detours, what she eventually said was that Ellen's departure was an unsolved mystery to her, too; and the interpretations she then proceeded to put on it were all of the most uncharitable kind.

A half-hour of her rambling speculations came to very little. All she actually knew was that Ellen had returned to the *pension,* paid her bill, packed her belongings—Mrs. Hoffer said, "I've never seen a girl who had fewer possessions; it was almost as if she *expected* to have to run away in the night"—and left. The procedure, according to Mrs. Hoffer, took less than fifteen minutes.

And that was that. The end of my leads. The end, in many ways, of my life.

8

FROM then on, I had no choice but to follow Eider's suggestion. I waited.

No word came.

I did my job—without inspiration or fire—but adequately.

After six interminable months, I was ordered back to England. And then I made my third and last visit to the American office on Unter den Linden.

Except for its façade, nothing about the place was familiar. The girl at the desk, for instance, was new. At least, she wasn't the Miss Blakeley of six months before.

In reply to my question she looked blank for a minute and then said, "I don't know a Mr. Eider. I think there was a man here by that name at one time, but he left before I came. I've been here only eight weeks."

I was persistent. It took almost an hour, and I spoke to four people before I was introduced to a Mr. Russell. He took me into a rococo little ante-room that was decorated in a heavy-handed imitation of Botticelli. There, surrounded by the fluffy clouds painted on the walls and ceiling, he said, "Yes, Mr.—ah—Terrant. May I help you?"

He was a slight, pale, very young man. His shoulders were narrow, and his fair hair was thinning. Altogether a nondescript young man. For no conceivable reason, I didn't like him. I was tired, and my six-month period of frustration had done something, something enervating, to me. During that time I had achieved the subtle, unhappy acceptance of adulthood that some fortunate people never attain. I got up off the ridiculous little *petit point* chair he had waved me into and said, "No. Never mind." I made for the door.

Before I reached it Mr. Russell cleared his throat and said, "Ah, Mr. Terrant—"

I turned around. He suddenly didn't look quite so nondescript. He looked, instead, sympathetic and upset.

He said, "Ah, Mr. Terrant, I shouldn't really discuss this with you, but you seem to have behaved quite discreetly these past months." At least, I thought, my indiscretions had not come to the attention of the Americans. "I am, ah, by way of being Mr. Eider's, ah, successor in this post. His records were—up-to-date—and so the facts are quite clear in my mind. It seems too bad to keep you, ah, waiting, as it were."

I came back into the room. "Yes?"

"Well—" Mr. Russell looked at his shoes, the ceiling, my shoes. He looked also as if he wished he had kept his mouth safely shut. He said, "Ah, yes. Well, you see, Miss Content never arrived in New York."

The words meant nothing to me. I said, "I beg your pardon?"

"She—ah—started for New York City just six months and three weeks ago—as you know, I believe. But she never arrived there. We have no reason to indulge in any hope that she is—ah—alive."

I said, "Thank you, Mr. Russell." There didn't seem to be anything else to say.

When I returned to London I wrote a letter, a long, comprehensive letter, to Washington. I laboured over it more carefully than any article I'd ever written. I took all the drama out of it, but it was a strong plea, just the same.

Until you face a situation such as the one I was staring at you can't imagine the difficulties a private citizen encounters. I didn't even know, for instance, to whom to address the letter. I finally sent it to "Central Intelligence Agency, Washington, D.C., U.S.A."

Then I waited again.

One evening about three weeks after I had posted the letter my door-bell rang. I found a short, stocky, pleasant-looking young man outside the door of my flat. He said, with a strong American accent, "Mr. Terrant?"

"Yes."

"May I speak to you a moment?"

"Certainly. Come in."

He came in, said his name was Benjamin, accepted a whisky and soda, sat in a comfortable armchair, and commented, with an engaging air of sincerity, that he admired my flat. Then he said, "I'm the answer to your letter to Washington."

I sat forward in my chair, eagerly, I expect, because he added gently, "Please, Mr. Terrant, don't be hopeful. This is a very distressing visit for me to have to pay, and for you to receive, I'm afraid. I've come to try to explain to you that we have nothing to tell you. That we are not holding out on you; that we just don't know anything. But I've been authorized to tell you exactly what we *do* know so you won't feel that we are—well—thwarting you.

"Ellen Content was flown here to London where she boarded a commercial ship. It had a rather mixed passenger list. Some returning American soldiers, some civilian personnel, some refugees, some English Army people bound for Washington. Miss Content was under a pseudonym, and she was offered no special protection because that seemed the best protection—that she seem as unimportant as possible. She was actually, as you may have guessed, *very* important—so much so that we had discarded our original idea of flying her home on the grounds that a ship was safer. And there was no trouble. The ship arrived on schedule—but Ellen Content wasn't on it. I think we may have bungled a little in our handling of the situation during the New York landing. In our anxiety to protect her by not making a fuss we permitted a lot of people to disembark and get out of reach before we clamped down and made a thorough search of the ship. She *may* have been smuggled off, but we think it unlikely. The chances are that she was lost at sea."

"Or perhaps taken off before the ship was well out of England?"

Mr. Benjamin hesitated. "That's possible. She had been instructed to be quiet and retiring, and she carried out those instructions so competently that no one, including the stewardess, seemed really aware of her presence. But really, Mr. Terrant, we have no hope. We think she was lost at sea."

9

THE day after Mr. Benjamin's visit I went into the managing editor's office and resigned.

There was a disconcerting silence after I had made my announcement. I don't know quite what I had expected—a plea for me to remain, perhaps; a show of temper; something. Instead, Deering just sat there and peered up at me in his short-sighted fashion.

Finally he said in a sober voice unlike his usual high-pitched, rather querulous tone, "Sit down, Terrant. No, not there"—as I made for the straight chair beside his desk—"over there." He got up from behind the desk and sat in one of the two leather armchairs that faced each other in front of the fireplace. I sat opposite him.

And, for a while, we just sat. I had said my piece. I couldn't imagine what there was left to say. But that was because I had been living in my own world, shut in all by myself, for half a year. I had never stopped to think that other people might have noticed that withdrawal.

Deering said, "What happened in Berlin?"

It took me by surprise. I said, "I'm sorry, sir. It's—not my story to tell."

"But something happened."

"To me, yes. And to—to people concerned with me. But not to the paper, or to my work, or—"

"Are you suggesting it's none of my business?" The voice was dry, but without its customary sharpness.

"Why, no." I hadn't been.

"Because it is my business, you know. Anything that affects the paper is my business. You are a good reporter"—I stared at him in amazement. He had never been known to pay a flat, outright compliment—"and the loss of you will affect the paper." He paused.

"I should say, you *were* a good reporter. Towards the end, in Berlin, you were—adequate, efficient—but not inspired. That quality of inspiration is what had previously set you above the rest. When I began to miss it, I questioned McConicky"—my superior in Berlin—"and he told me that something personal had, in his opinion, thrown you off base. He had no idea what it was."

I said inanely, "Yes, sir."

He glanced sharply at me, and then looked into the fire. After a minute he said, in rather a changed voice, "All right, then. But I'd suggest you try free-lancing."

I was surprised. "But you don't like—"

"I know. I know! But I just told you, I'm usually concerned only with the good of this paper. Free-lance stuff is of no use to us. But it does have its purposes, and you would be unusually effective. Your abilities lie in trends; you seem to spy them out. You have an instinct for research and follow up. That makes for good free-lance pieces. D'you know Nigel Lamson?"

I don't think I had ever heard him mention a rival editor before. I said, "Yes. Very well. We served together a bit of the time."

"Yes. Well, he's an old, uh, acquaintance of mine, too. I'll put in a word. *His* sheet"—there was infinite scorn in the words—"fills up columns with the sort of thing you could give dignity to."

"Well, thank you very much." It was an excellent suggestion, and one that might not have occurred to me. After all, I had to eat, and would have to do some work. But it would have been impossible to continue to accept a weekly salary when I intended to put so much time into my search for Ellen. Besides, as he said, the inspiration was gone. The work had become secondary, and the paper was not getting value.

What I did not know then, although I imagine Deering suspected it, was that as a free-lancer I would earn far more money for far less work—and for work that suited me better, at that.

We both looked into the fire, and then I said again, "Well, thank you, sir—" and started to rise.

He said irritably, "Just a minute, just a minute."

I sank back into the chair.

"About this problem of yours, this *personal* problem—is there any way I can help?" He added hastily, "Not prying, you know. But if it's health, I might know a doctor, if it's money, there may be a solution, if it's love—" He threw up his hands and looked at me with a wry, embarrassed, deprecating smile.

Perhaps he *could* help me. I said slowly, "It's beyond all that—that's what makes it so difficult. I can't proceed honestly—go to the doctor, as it were. It seems I have to—Look, sir, if I used the phrase in copy you'd probably chuck me out, but it really comes under the heading of 'international intrigue.'"

His face didn't change very much, but I had known him for a long time—I would say he was astounded. He finally asked, rather sharply, "In which you are involved?"

"Not directly. But someone I—love—is very directly involved."

"Culpable?"

"No. Patriot."

"Ah, well, then perhaps I *can* help. Unless you have a more specific way, go to see this chap. He may be quite helpful."

He went over to his desk, scrawled a few words on a piece of yellow copy paper, and handed the paper to me.

It said, "Divisional Superintendent Daniel Jelliffson, Special Branch, Scotland Yard."

I don't think I would have got to see Superintendent Jelliffson, even presuming I had known he existed, without using Deering's name. I'd have been shunted off to an assistant. As it was, when I was ushered into his office at the exact second of my telephone-made appointment, I had been made acutely aware that he was a busy man and that I had better come directly to the point. So I did.

"I've come to you, on Colonel Marriott Deering's advice, about a missing person."

He was a big man, surprisingly typical of the Yard's inhabitants—square, broad, with an impassive, plain face that had no trace of individuality in any of its features. When he spoke his voice, too, was quite typical. Strong voice, good accent, but not public school. "Are you certain you are in the right place? Perhaps you want the Missing Persons Branch?"

"This seems to involve America, Russia, and perhaps Germany."

He looked directly at me, but his impassivity was intact. "Not Great Britain?"

"I don't know about that. I think not, but—Well, I thought, America, you know, allies—"

"Who is the missing person?"

"Her name was—*is*—Ellen Content. American. A member of their—"

Rather surprisingly, he interrupted me. "And your interest?"

I stretched the truth a trifle. "I was—*am* engaged to marry Miss Content."

Jelliffson stared at me without expression for a minute, and I braced myself for the next question, but none came. Instead he rose and said, "Please return here tomorrow at the same time. Will that be convenient?"

I said in bewilderment, "Yes, but—"

The Superintendent raised his eyebrows. "But—?"

"I'll be here tomorrow."

For my second appointment, the same timing was observed. I fancied I could hear the tower clock chiming the hour as I entered the Superintendent's office. I took the same seat and faced the same dispassionate regard. It seemed as if the twenty-four hours had not passed. But they had, as the Divisional Superintendent made clear to me instantly.

He said, "I asked you to give me a day's lapse so I could familiarize myself with the details of the case." He paused. "And, of course, to ascertain whether or not we actually consider it a 'case.'"

That sounded technical and unintelligible to me. I waited.

"Now, please tell me exactly what you know about the disappearance of Ellen Content. In detail, please."

Well, I had had twenty-four hours, too. In detail, omitting all high lights but none of the facts, I told him of the Berlin series of events. As a result of my night's practice, it took me no more than three minutes.

When I had finished, he said, "Yes. In other words, you know nothing the authorities don't know."

I had never thought of it that way, and I didn't see the relevance of the remark. "Why, no, I don't. Of course I don't. In fact"—I thought it over for a second—"one could say I know *nothing,* and leave it at that. Presumably the Americans have more information about the reasons for and facts surrounding Ellen's disappearance, but, you see, that doesn't interest me. All I want is Ellen Content—not information. I'm not trying to solve anything; I'm not interested in the matter as a politician, or a newspaper reporter, or—"

"Rather selfish, don't you think?"

I stared at him with my mouth still open.

"It seems to me that you are blindly determined to pursue one woman without regard for the consequences or any of the possible results to—others."

I was so far back on my heels I couldn't get my balance. I asked in sheer bewilderment, "*What* consequences? *What* others? Did you get me to tell you the details of my association with Miss Content just to find out what I might know—without thought of helping—"

"The Americans have repeatedly—according to your own story—requested you not to meddle. And, again according to your own story, you have just as repeatedly ignored them."

A feeling of vast unreality was coming over me. The only clear emotion that broke through was that I disliked Superintendent Jelliffson more than I had ever disliked anyone in my life. With a fury that did not seep into my voice—I noticed with astonishment that I succeeded in sounding merely stiff—I said, "I am not an American. I do not owe loyalty—"

Jelliffson stood up. He said, "I do not know the whereabouts of Ellen Content. So, if it gives you any satisfaction to have the answer you came for—there it is. But here is an additional fact—

command—call it what you will: the Americans, as you pointed out yesterday, are our friends; you will please heed their requests in the future. To add weight to it, consider this: His Majesty's Government now states that you are to desist from your inquiries."

I was dismissed.

10

As I sat in Gander a little more than a year after my conversation with Divisional Superintendent Jelliffson, I found that my dislike of him had not been tempered by time. Nor was the recollection sweetened by the memory of the fact that, because I had been so dumbfounded by his unexpected attack, I had made no further protest, had marched out of his office in a blind but ignominiously silent rage.

And, thereafter, my hands had been tied. I soon discovered that Colonel Deering had sent me to the right man in the first place, and there was no other port of call.

Because despite Jelliffson's injunction, I tried. I mercilessly used every friend, every associate, every nodding acquaintance I could dig up. I pulled strings, "saw" people, cajoled, threatened, and traded favours. But the few leads that came of those efforts were futile and thwarting because all agencies and individuals turned out to be merely rungs on the ladder—some of them high, some of them low, but all leading to Jelliffson on the top rung.

And so I had sat silent for that year as I was sitting now in Gander—part of the time in revolt, fury, agony; the remainder and increasingly larger part of the time in resignation and dull pain.

From the moment I had seen Ellen's name in *The Times* until my arrival in Gander I had been in such precipitate motion that I had not had time to come to the realization that for the first time since he issued it I was actively flouting Jelliffson's order—and to a greater degree than when he issued it, since, as a result of the Korean "police action," we had for a few weeks now been working allies of the

Americans. It's true that I had made every effort to go against his instructions, but I had got nowhere. Now I was in decisive motion.

I must admit that the thought gave me, disloyally enough, more satisfaction than discomfort. Jelliffson be damned—all I cared about, all I prayed for, was that my surmise was correct and that Ellen was now on the *Elizabeth,* steaming briskly towards America. But not too briskly, because I began to fear we'd not make New York in time to meet the boat.

We left Gander at six-thirty in the morning and arrived at the International Airport at eighty-forty—nine-forty Daylight Saving Time. My first question to the dour-looking customs man was, "Has the *Queen Elizabeth* docked yet?"

He looked blank.

"The *Elizabeth,* man! The ship. The steamer."

He still looked blank. Then he said, "Oh, the *Queen Elizabeth.* How should I know? My business is planes, and I have more than enough trouble with them."

"Well, may I please get through to a telephone and find out of she's in yet?"

"You can't communicate with anyone until you have cleared through customs."

"Well, *clear* me then!"

That was a mistake. He was an elderly man, crotchety and over-officious. I'd put his back up, and in retaliation he saw to it that I underwent the most thorough search possible. He examined my single rather small suitcase for a false bottom, which the naked eye accepted as a flat impossibility, and for a while I thought he was going to insist upon a search of my person.

Then when he finally let me go I was held up at the exit by a pleasant-looking young man, who must have thought me very rude. He said, "Mr. Terrant?"

"Yes." I was straining to pass him.

He stepped out of my path, but he looked confused. He said hastily, in an effort to hold me, "I'm Baylor, of the paper's New York office. I'm here—"

I didn't feel the need of a welcoming committee. I was three feet beyond him and backing away as I cut in: "Yes, yes, Mr. Baylor. Can I do something for you?"

He stared at me in bewilderment. "Well, no, not exactly. I've come to do something for—I mean, I've brought you the expense money authorized by—"

"Ah, yes. Thanks."

I snatched the envelope out of his hand and sped through the airport in search of a telephone booth, leaving him with his hand outstretched and his mouth open.

But a minute later I regretted his loss.

You know, I'd never been in the States. I didn't understand the telephone books. I stared at a rack of thick books marked Westchester, Manhattan (I understood that well enough to think it was of no use to me), Brooklyn (which, until that moment, had stood for an incomprehensible joke to me), and so on. I finally pleaded with a passing lady who thought the whole thing rather a lark, but outside of some quite unnecessary amusement, got through to the steamship line for me in short order.

In response to my question, the operator said, "Yes, sir. The *Elizabeth* docked at nine-eleven."

"Thank you. What is the address of the pier?"

She told me. I ran through the airport into the unbelievable heat beyond, leaped in a taxi, and gave the driver the address. He had a distressing tendency to talk, and that, combined with the heat, which, because of the car's low roof, seemed to be pressing down on me, and the terrible traffic we encountered after we had ridden for about half an hour, gave me a feeling of impotent urgency.

When I finally reached the dock, I ploughed through the frightful crowds, rode the slowest escalator I'd ever mounted, and came eventually to the gate. But my path in every direction was paved with stumbling blocks of one shape or another. It seemed that I would not be permitted to go beyond the high wooden gate until every individual had cleared through the customs. And that, the uniformed man at the gate advised me frankly but cheerfully would be hours. My urgency must have communicated itself to him to some degree because he finally suggested that perhaps he could get a customs guard to come and talk to me.

"I'd appreciate it tremendously," I told him. "The guard at 'C' Division, please."

The customs guard was a pleasant, intelligent man. He really tried to be helpful. Yes, he said, he remembered the name. A pretty name for a pretty young lady. Yes, Miss Content had cleared through the customs. She was one of the first people through. No, of course, he had no way of knowing where she had gone, but—wait a minute—he could tell me who had carried her luggage. It was that porter there.

"Hey, Jimmy!" he called.

The guard from "C" went off and left me to Jimmy, a lanky Negro, who was also kind and anxious to be helpful. He said he knew the name of the cab driver he had turned Miss Content over to, just by coincidence, he added. It was unusual for him to know those boys by name, but this one often came to the docks for arrivals.

"And what is his name?"

"Joe."

"Joe what?"

"Oh, I don't know that."

The man guarding the gate had been an interested spectator. Now he decided to help out. "What kind of a cab does he drive?" he asked the porter.

"A Sunbeam."

The guard said to me, "Well, mister, that isn't too bad. You just call the Sunbeam people and tell them you want to talk to the driver of one of their cabs who stopped at this pier at about nine-thirty this morning. Then they'll ask each guy as he checks in." He turned to the porter again. "What's this Joe look like?"

"Oh, he's just about average. He's coloured."

The guard beamed. "Now, there you are, mister. He shouldn't be too hard for them to weed out. Especially if you promise to take care of 'em."

That reminded me of my manners. I "took care" of the two men out of the envelope, and went back to the street, where, by a process of doubling in half, I crawled under the roof of a cab. I explained to the driver that I wanted a big, commercial, centrally located hotel, and he chauffeured me to one that was built right over the big railway terminal, Grand Central Station.

I registered at the big main desk and was escorted up to a small room that looked like a comfortable version of all the anonymous rooms ever furnished. As soon as the bellboy considered me installed and had departed, I made for the telephone. I told the hotel operator to connect me with the Sunbeam Taxicab Company. That manoeuvre saved me the problem of telephone books.

The Sunbeam dispatcher was helpful and hopeful. Any of their cabs on the street at that hour, he said, would probably check in about five o'clock that afternoon (I looked at my watch; it was then eleven-thirty) and it wouldn't be any problem at all to question the drivers as they reported in.

"Besides," he added, "I'm pretty sure which guy it is. I know a coloured guy named Joe among that crew. You just leave your number and sit tight. I'll find out where the young lady went, and then I'll call you right back."

People seemed very nice. On the strength of that conclusion I telephoned downstairs and asked to have a bellboy sent up to my room. When he arrived, I explained my ignorance of phone books, and he launched into an explanation.

I learned that New York City is a matter of locution: it is the whole, and it is one of five parts of the whole. This threw my conservative Euclidean mind into some confusion. I also learned that, in its one-fifth version, it is the largest part; but so is Brooklyn. This last he then reduced to temporary intelligence by explaining that, again confounding Euclid, we had been dealing in disparate terms: Brooklyn is the largest in *area*; Manhattan is the largest in *population*.

"Manhattan?"

"New York City."

"Ah, then, the terms are synonymous."

"Huh?"

"The terms 'New York City' and 'Manhattan' mean the same thing."

"Yeah, that's it."

"Then applying the words 'New York City' to Manhattan is merely a matter of usage? In addressing a letter for instance, one would correctly write 'Manhattan?'"

"Naw. NewYork, New York, ya gotta write."

I gave that up. "However," I said, climbing back on to what I thought was firmer ground, "Manhattan has the largest population?"

"Yeah. But not living population."

I stared at him. "Dead population?" I ventured.

"No, no. I mean they work here, but they don't live here. At night everybody goes to the other boroughs, mostly Brooklyn, or to other states, mostly Jersey."

This drew a transportation picture that strained my imagination. It also depressed me, and I moved quickly out of it and fastened on the word he had used. "So you call these five parts boroughs?"

"Yeah. Come to think of it, though, we call 'em counties, too."

I must have looked confused because he added, "You see, Manhattan is New York County—"

"Ah," I interrupted. "*That*'s where the double terminology first arose!"

"Huh? Oh, I see what you mean." He examined the thought and then said dubiously, "Well, I dunno. You see, while Queens is Queens County, Brooklyn is Kings County—"

My despair must have shown on my face, because he said, "Look, I guess I'm no teacher. You wanna map?"

I thought that was a splendid idea, and he went out and purchased a map of Greater New York City for me.

The map cleared up the physical aspects of the city, but the terminology will never have any real intelligence for me. Manhattan is Manhattan, and rarely Manhattan Island; but Staten is never Staten, and *always* Staten Island. Part of Long Island is Brooklyn, but Brooklyn is not part of Long Island. "The Bronx" is customary usage, but "The Richmond" would, it seems, be a joke.

Some of the sympathy I had always felt for the bewildered New Yorkers who wandered around London evaporated. Indeed, our pronunciations are arbitrary and quite confusing, but the New Yorkers' plaintive criticisms of them seemed less justified.

The map and my speculations served a useful purpose. They took up time. And I had plenty of time, and I had to spend it in that hotel room. I sat in that room, ate in that room, and, eventually, slept for a while.

And, as the day slowly passed, I felt a renewal of the hope I had almost lost in Gander. For the first time, the first time in almost two years, a coincidence had helped me: the porter knew the cab driver. Maybe that was the usual situation in New York City, maybe the drivers kept to regular beats, but it seemed an unlikely eventuality to me. I preferred to accept it as a sign from Providence that some good fortune would attend my efforts.

I think, now, that I was whistling to myself in my dark air tunnel, because another dreadful thought was trying to get through to my conscious mind. I had been steadfastly refusing to recognize its existence since the moment, only one day before, when I had read the words "Ellen Content" in *The Times*.

At five-thirty the telephone interrupted my speculations. It was the Sunbeam dispatcher, and he didn't sound nearly so cheerful as he had earlier in the day.

"I'm afraid, mister—"

"What's the matter?"

"Well, he got away from me. I don't understand it. One minute I was looking out for him, and then before I even turned around there was his hack and his card was signed in. I just can't understand how it could have happened—"

"Well, it happened. What do we do now?"

"Do now?"

"How do I find him? What steps do I take? What do I *do?*" I checked myself. I think I'm a patient man, but Mr. Eider hadn't thought so two years before in Berlin. The customs guard hadn't thought so that morning. The provocation of years wouldn't interest the Sunbeam dispatcher, but rudeness, abruptness, might throw him into reverse, as it had the customs official.

I said carefully, "I really must reach that driver. Is there anything you can think of that might help me?"

"He'll be on duty around eight o'clock tomorrow morning." He did sound stiff.

I said, "No. That would be a most difficult delay for me. Tell you what—if you can find him for me tonight I'll be glad to send you fifty dollars, and you can divide it between yourself and the driver as you see fit."

Fifty dollars sounded like a respectable sum. It was not until we had disconnected that I discovered it came to over £17—very respectable indeed.

There was a short pause. Then, with a careful repression of jubilance that showed he, too, considered it respectable, he said. "Now, that's very nice of you. Well, I could look up his employment record and try to reach him at his home."

I said thanks, went back to the bed, and stared unseeingly at the ceiling. It seemed to me that my gratitude for the coincidence could be considered cancelled out.

In a half-hour the dispatcher called back. The driver had no home phone number listed on his employment form.

"Well, telegraph him."

"A wire? Okay, but he lives in Harlem. Deliveries are pretty slow up there. It'll probably take some time. I'll tell him to call at my home because the whole story'd be too hard to explain in a wire. Okay, I'll try it."

It was a little after eleven that night before the phone rang again. What had been going on in my mind during those six hours is not pleasant to recall.

When I lifted the receiver a soft, cheerful voice told me, before I could ask, that he was Joe, that he had heard I was asking about a young lady.

I said, "Yes, I—"

"Of the *Elizabeth,* huh?"

"Yes, she—"

"Her name was Comfort—something like that—and she was tall and blonde?"

My pause was almost imperceptible. Then I said, "Yes."

"What did you want to know, sir?"

"I want to find her. I was—uh—bringing her good news, and I missed the landing."

"That's easy. She was a foreigner, and she was sure lost. First she went up to the St. Regis Hotel. She was only in there maybe two, three minutes and then she came out and said she wanted to get to Albany. She didn't know a *thing,* and I hadda help her out. I got a red cap, and together we put her on the ten o'clock to Troy. On the New York Central."

To me, Troy was Ilium, and it conjured up the topless towers that Helen was responsible for razing. I said, "But I thought you said she wanted to go to Albany?" That, too, sounded as if it had come out of the Shakespearian period.

"Well, the next train to Albany wasn't until noon. She didn't wanna wait. So she went to Troy, and then she was gonna take a bus back. It's only a coupla miles, and there's a regular bus service between Troy and Albany."

"I see. Well, thank you."

"She was very nice. Very generous."

"Yes. I've arranged with the Sunbeam dispatcher to be generous, too. See him in the morning."

"Thank *you,* sir."

11

PERHAPS I should have flown. I don't know, to this minute, if it would have been possible. The clerk at the hotel desk took over for me and booked me on a train that left at 2.35 a.m. and was to arrive in Albany at 6.20 in the morning. He explained that it was the last train and that I was lucky to get on it.

As I addressed an envelope to the dispatcher, care of the Sunbeam Taxicab Company, and tucked five ten-dollar bills inside, I thought of men and gambles. The dispatcher, on a gamble, had put in a number of hours and his own money for a telegram. The gamble was now paying off for him.

Would I be as lucky in my larger gamble?

The clerk had said I was lucky to get on that train, and perhaps I was, but I didn't find it a happy ride. "Tall and blonde." The words kept echoing through my mind. The dreadful thought—the knowledge, really—that had been in the back of my consciousness had been graphically confirmed by the cabby. A tall blonde who was going to "fill a series of dancing engagements" was not Ellen. It is possible for a woman to turn blonde in far less than two years but the *petite* Ellen certainly hadn't turned tall. And Ellen was a school-teacher—not a dancer. The woman going by the name of Ellen Content was probably Natasha. Though even that was presumption. It could have been anyone, anyone in the wide world.

But I didn't feel that I was on a wild-goose chase. Someone was going about under the name of Ellen Content. It was a lead—to where, to what, I didn't know. But it was a lot more of a lead than I'd had a few days earlier.

51

By the light of the pinpoint beam thrown from over my chair I studied the map of New York State I had purchased in Grand Central Station—the bellboy had planted a good habit in me. Albany was the capital of New York State, a vast state to my surprised British eyes. Albany was located on the Hudson River, about a hundred and fifty miles due north of New York City, and it had about the same population as Norwich. I made a savage X on the map. The map didn't tell me why the blonde was travelling to Albany, what she could possibly want in a city as small as Norwich.

All that could be said about Albany at 6.20 on a July morning was that it was oppressively hot. If it was that hot in the early morning. . . .

A cab driver guided me to the De Witt Clinton Hotel, where I had a piece of luck. Or so I thought. What I didn't realize was that the De Witt Clinton was *the* large commercial hotel—the place to which strangers automatically trekked.

The clerk at the hotel desk, a yawning, pince-nezed, tight-faced little man, didn't like me. He may merely have been tired or he may have had an aversion to the British; whatever his reasons, he didn't like me. However, to my question he admitted grudgingly that Ellen Content had checked into the De Witt Clinton at about two-thirty on the afternoon of the previous day.

"What's her room number?"

He gave me a cold stare. "We wouldn't dream of giving out such information about a lady."

I was carefully polite. "Well, how would a person reach her?"

"You'd telephone and ask for her."

"Oh. Well, where are the house phones?"

"They're *right* beside you, sir. *Right* there on that ledge." He waited until I had almost reached the bank of phones on a ledge beside the desk before he added, "But Miss Content checked out less than an hour ago."

I untensed my muscles and said evenly, "Thank you. Can you perhaps tell me what her business was in Albany?"

"I *beg* your pardon."

I gave it up.

I was escorted to my room by a young bellboy who distinctly and happily remembered Miss Content.

"She checked out not much more than a half-hour ago. She was—very pretty, sir. I sure wouldn't be likely to forget *her*. She spoke like a foreigner, but a real *interesting* foreigner."

I got the idea. The girl sounded more and more like Natasha. "Do you know where she went?"

"Yeah. She went to the station."

"The railroad station? Do you know what train she took?"

He shook his head. "I wouldn't know that. But there's only two trains she coulda took. There's a six-twenty-three to New York. And there's a six-twenty going the other way—towards Niagara Falls. You musta just got off one of them. I'd say she was the New York type."

I sat in my second anonymous room and faced facts. My impotence, my unsuitability for the task at hand was glaring. I was not a detective. I was not a tracer of missing persons. I did not even consider myself particularly ingenious at deducing things. And I had a vast lack of knowledge about my locale. But what could I do? Hire a detective? Well, I suppose I could have. But I had no idea how much that would cost in money or entail in time. And both were running out. I didn't see how I could go to the police—I even suspected I might be on the wrong side of the law. Was it permissible to track people down from city to city? Probably, but certainly the police weren't going to *help* me do it without checking, and—it seemed hopeless.

So there was nothing for it: I was left to the job of deducing. According to *The Times,* "Ellen Content" had sailed to New York to "fill a series of dancing engagements." Without complicating matters, then, it would seem that she had danced in the small city of Albany. If I didn't ask myself why in heaven's name she should do any such thing, if I didn't cloud my mind with the realization of my impotency, perhaps I could still find her. I remembered the remark Colonel Deering had made the day I resigned from the paper: "You have an instinct for research and follow up." I hoped he was right on the follow-up part.

No place that offered entertainment in the evenings was likely to be open at seven in the morning, so I made a successful effort to sleep. At noon, armed with a list of likely places through the cooperation of the pleasant—very pleasant, by contrast—day clerk, I started along Albany's State Street.

I soon discovered that no place that had entertainment was any farther open at noon than it had been at 7 a.m. I also discovered that Albany was a city of hills—steep hills. And the morning's promise of heat had been amply fulfilled.

And so, steaming in my inappropriate tweeds, feeling inefficient, feeling certain that there was something I could be doing that I hadn't been clever enough to think up, I returned to my hotel room and contained myself until late afternoon, when I started out again.

I hit it on my third try. The manager of The Blue Lily said, Certainly. Miss Ellen Content had been the feature dancer in his floor show the night before.

"And very good, too. I offered her a two-week engagement. But she said she couldn't; had a tour all arranged. I think she'd a been worth it. I coulda done some fast advertising and, anyway, word woulda got around. Even her picture on the billboard outside woulda brought in business."

I felt more of my weight transfer itself to my left elbow, which was propped on the small bar in the entrance corridor of the little night club.

"Her picture? You had a photograph of Ellen Content?"

"But, sure!" Mr. Dimitrios opened wide his very black eyes and spread his very stubby arms in one combined expansive gesture. "I got three pictures. I can't engage anyone without some idea of what I'm gettin.' Though—I tell you this confidential, because it seems maybe like you're romantically looking for the very nice young lady—"

I endeavoured to look romantic, but succeeded in feeling more stiffly British than I had before. It occurred to me that the romance lay in Mr. Dimitrios' Greek forebears rather than in any impression I had given.

"—So, confidential I explain to you: it was an unusual engage-ment. Miss Content, she danced for nothing."

Mr. Dimitrios seemed to expect a large gesture of surprise or exclamation of astonishment from me, so I obliged by repeating weakly, "For nothing?"

He seemed satisfied with my attempt. "For nothing!" He nodded his head so vigorously that the shining black waves fell forward into a cluster of curls. "It was like this: a week, a coupla weeks ago, I receive a letter from Paris—Paris, yet!—explaining that Miss Content wants to try to dance in the United States, but doesn't know if her style of dancing would be good here, if people would like it. She offers she should come and dance—for nothing!—on the night of July fifteenth.

"Well, me, I got a business. This ain't a amateur-night spot or something. I can't gamble on getting someone funny in here. But she encloses these three pictures, see. And—wow! So I figure that on her figure alone I can't lose nothing. And I return the self-addressed envelope and say yes, to come on."

I leaned more heavily on the bar and took a very deep breath. "Mr. Dimitrios, do you still have that letter?"

"Aw, no. I don't have no secretary. The hat-check girl takes care of those things, and she's not very smart. So I find it easiest to throw papers away as soon as I can."

Mr. Dimitrios must have found some expression of regret in my face or in his imperfect understanding of the situation because he added, "That makes you unhappy?" His face moved easily into a network of downward lines. "Would you like maybe to see the pictures? Ah, that makes you happy! Well, I don't like to give up anything so beautiful, so I won't give them to you, but I'll show them to you."

He called imperiously to the bartender, "John! Give the gentleman a drink." And to me, "I'll be right back. You make yourself comfortable, have a drink."

The bartender, a slenderer and even darker version of Mr. Dimitrios, gave me a whisky and soda, and I sat, with my elbows on the bar, praying over the drink.

Mr. Dimitrios was indeed right back. With him he brought three pictures of Natasha—a Natasha even more exotic and glamorous than the one I had met. She was arrayed in several beads, and

I realized that poor Ed Bigeby had had a better X-ray eye than I—or perhaps merely a greater interest. Natasha's figure was almost beyond compare. His term and his voice came back to me: Natasha was "a dish." But she looked younger than she had when I met her two years before.

Mr. Dimitrios voiced my thoughts. "Like all theatrical pictures I guess these were taken quite a long while ago. Theatricals!" He spread his arms again, this time outward and upward, and this time he accompanied the motion with his lips, exposing a dazzling set of perfect teeth. "But the young lady now is, if such a thing is possible, even more beautiful. I guess you know, huh?"

I nodded limply.

"Why don't you go after her? You come so far, so you go a little farther, huh?"

I transferred my gaze from the pictures to Mr. Dimitrios's beaming, romantic face.

He said, "Syracuse, it's not so far, no?"

I shook my head, though I had no conception of where Syracuse was. To me, it spoke of ancient Syracusae, as Troy had of Ilium. It occurred to me that the old Greek word sat well on Mr. Dimitrios's lips—better than almost anything else he had said.

When I could trust my voice, I said, "Yes, I think that's a good idea. I'll go to Syracuse. But do you know where in Syracuse?"

"Sure! I tried to talk Miss Content into staying here and she said no, she had an engagement to dance in Syracuse in—What was the name of the joint?" He thumped his forehead heavily. "Ah, yes! The Gaslight Club, that was it!"

12

On the train on the way to Syracuse I moodily made another X on my map. I travelled another hundred and fifty miles, this time to the west and slightly north, and in that pleasant town that so unfittingly bore the name of a place of ancient battle, of pestilence, blockade, and oblivion, I repeated my experience of Albany—incident by incident.

Miss Content had stayed at the Hotel Syracuse, as did I, and just as briefly.

The Gaslight Club was in Salina Street.

Miss Content had danced at The Gaslight Club.

Mr. Ben Green of The Gaslight Club, a gentleman slightly less swarthy, slightly more literate, and slightly stubbier than Mr. Dimitrios, was just as helpful as Mr. Dimitrios and perhaps as sentimental. I say "perhaps" because, having learned my lesson, I fed Mr. Green romance in large doses, and he wasn't put to the test to devise a story for me. He reacted instantly. Miss Content, who had sent him the same three pictures and the same letter as Mr. Dimitrios had received, had made an undying impression on him. He regretted her loss and wished me better luck. She had left his club at four o'clock that morning and was proceeding immediately to Utica. He didn't know where in Utica she would dance, but, he assured me, it was a comparatively small town (about half the population of Syracuse, I later learned, and everything is indeed relative), and I should have no trouble finding her.

I went to Utica by bus, and I travelled in a triumphant mood.

It was early evening. Utica (which conjured up ancient
Carthage—I was getting heartily sick of the historical allusions) was
only fifty miles due east of Syracuse. A mere couple of hours. Natasha
would not have had time to do her dancing act and get out of Utica.
She probably would not even have set out for whatever scrubby
little night club she had chosen in that town. My dreary double
experience must now be at an end. Whatever happened, it couldn't
be in the pattern of Albany and Syracuse.

And it wasn't. It was worse. It was blood and thunder again, as
it had been in Berlin. Blood and thunder, which I am constitutionally
unequipped to deal with.

I entered the lobby of the Utica Hotel shortly after nine that evening.
I left my luggage—my single suitcase that had been almost unopened—
on the rubber mat in front of the hotel. As I went through the
double doors of the hotel the doorman was whistling vigorously for
a boy to carry it inside.

I approached the desk confidently. The clerk and I exchanged a
few comments about the weather—it struck me that everyone in
New York State seemed to be as surprised as I by the almost unbear-
able heat, but I had a deep and unreasonable intuitive feeling that
everyone was bluffing, that it was often that hot in July, but that no
one would admit it. Then as the clerk—a very young man—started
to turn the desk contraption that held the registration card towards
me, I asked, "Is a Miss Ellen Content registered here?"

I reached for the pen, but it was awkwardly out of my grasp. After
a second the surprising fact that the clerk was frozen to the pad got
through to me. I looked up and found that the boy's face had turned
to a mask of surprise. His eyes were held wide and round, his mouth
was set in the circle of a wordless "ooo."

He said, "*You* know her? They'll want to talk to you! Right
where you are standing. This morning. Practically where you are
standing. A little bit over that way." He waved towards his left.
"I heard the shot, but—"

A tall, spare, dry-looking man in a stiff collar moved up behind
the boy. "That's all right, Mr. Nelson," he said. Although he spoke

sharply, there was a fatherly note of reassurance in his voice. "If you'll sort those cards, I'll take care of this gentleman."

The boy said, "Cards? Oh," and moved round the partition the key racks formed behind the desk. The stiff-looking man turned to me and said, "Now, Mr.—?"

I didn't answer. I wasn't attempting to evade—not yet—but I hadn't caught up quite, and I was feeling a little shocked. After the days of nothing . . . But the manager must have read something into my silence. He said, as soothingly as his dry voice and stiff exterior permitted, "The young lady is doing fine. She's safely in Memorial Hospital. Now, if you'll just sign the register"—he turned the forgotten register pad towards me—"I'll see to it that someone comes and—tells you all about the incident."

Still feeling blank and shocked, I took the pen out of its holder. He murmured something, and followed the young man into the behind-the-scenes.

Then I caught up. He was phoning.

I put the pen neatly back into its holder and turned and walked to the door. Outside, the doorman looked guilty; after having whistled frantically for my benefit, he was now talking leisurely to the boy who had answered his summons. The boy reached hastily down for my suitcase's handle, but I beat him to it.

"Perfectly all right," I said. "I'll walk part of the way."

The *non sequitur* threw them into the momentary confusion I had hoped for. It seemed a long way to the corner but I took it slowly. When I had turned it, I started to run.

At nine o'clock in Utica in mid-July it is not quite dark. The dusk isn't like England's, however. It doesn't stretch on and on until almost eleven o'clock at night. By nine-thirty, it is thoroughly dark. At nine-thirty I sat at a terrible little counter in a very dirty, very small counter-restaurant. It was only ten minutes or so since I had rounded the corner of the hotel, but it seemed as if hours had passed, and I felt that I had travelled miles.

Why had I run? Why was I running?

I struggled with the answers. If Natasha had been shot I would be hopelessly detained. Under such conditions, even the English police would hold one up indefinitely, and—if one was to credit the movies and fiction on the subject—the American police were far less considerate. There was no question of my being accused of shooting Natasha—it would be extremely easy to have Mr. Green testify to my presence in Syracuse—but there was equally little likelihood of my being permitted to continue my search.

All right. Then I had to run. But where? I had reached the end. I had reached, or almost reached—Natasha.

But I had wanted Ellen.

Who could help me?

Well, maybe Natasha could.

The stiff man behind the Utica's desk had said she was in Memorial Hospital. Memorial Hospital, then. Would the police, who were undoubtedly looking for me by now, look there? Probably, but perhaps not yet. By staying at the hotel desk I could have found out about Natasha. I hadn't stayed there, so they might logically assume, for a bit, at any rate, that my interest lay in escaping Utica, not in entering Memorial Hospital.

But they *would* be looking for me. What would they look for? It struck me that, in a way, I presented an appearance which it was almost impossible to define. I was a bit above average height, but beyond that I should be quite difficult to describe. My most distinctive quality, it seemed to me, was a negative one. I looked *quieter* than most of the Americans I had seen; blander, more self-effacing, more . . .

I gave it up. Whatever the quality was, if I couldn't put a word to it myself, how would the desk clerk manage to?

But there was one betraying factor: my accent. I had been watching heads turn and eyes change expression every time I spoke since my brush with the customs official at the airport. Some looked surprised, some looked intrigued, some looked elaborately normal, but no one failed to mark the accent. So every time I opened my mouth I would give myself away. And it was unlikely that the small city of Utica contained very many Englishmen.

I pondered that for a while. I came up with what, I'm afraid, was a rather asinine solution: I would have a toothache.

I started with the man behind the counter. So far all I had said to him was "Coffee." Now I clamped my hand over my right lower jaw, moved my lips as little as possible, and mumbled, "Can you tell me where Memorial Hospital is?"

I thought the sounds gratifyingly uncharacteristic. The meaning barely got through, and no accent seemed to accompany it. The man started towards me, delayed to take money from the only other customer in the place, and then, as the customer left, said, "Sure. But that's no place to go for a toothache."

"More than a toothache. Surgery," I muttered. It seemed silly, but possible.

"Oh. Well, you go down two blocks"—he waved—"and then up five. You can't miss it. It's a big, square, five-storey building—only one that big around there."

13

I STOOD in the street opposite Memorial Hospital and looked helplessly at it. I had no plan. It seemed extremely unlikely that they would let me see Natasha—it was nighttime, it was her first day in hospital, I was not a relative. Besides, I had no assurance that Natasha was conscious and in talking condition. Well, I would simply have to hope that she was not too ill to talk. And having formulated that prayer, I then had the further problem—how to get to her? I finally decided on the direct approach, I had no other.

I placed my suitcase under the steps of a private house, crossed the street, and walked through the swinging doors that led into the lighted reception room of the hospital. There I had my first surprise. I was all alone in a small, bright entrance room, which was all white and pale-green paint. Ahead of me there was a small area, enclosed by a railing, that held a desk, a switchboard, and a swivel chair. The chair was moving slightly. Obviously a receptionist usually sat there, but had just left his or her post.

On the railing in front of the chair lay an opened book, a ledger kind of book. I turned it towards me, and there it was. Simple as that. The left page was headed "AM Admissions," the right page, "PM Admissions." The second name on the left page was "Ellen Content." There were a number of notes after the name, but they didn't exist for me because in the farthest right column was neatly pencilled the much more interesting information—"Room 203."

I passed no one on the stairs. But, I reminded myself, ten o'clock is late in a hospital. Perhaps the situation was not so unusual as it seemed, after all.

The second-storey lights were dimmed. As I reached the top of the stairway I saw my first living being in that sterile place. Going away from me down the darkened corridor was a man. As I climbed the last step he turned a corner and was out of sight.

Room 203 was the second door on the right. The only thing that broke the monotonous symmetry of the corridor was the empty straight chair beside the door of that room.

I took a deep breath and opened the door slowly.

The room was small, stark-white, and dimly lit. There was almost no furniture, little to distract me from the one important thing the room contained—Natasha Paviloff. She lay quietly, her head slightly raised by her pillows. Her face was colourless, frighteningly so, and her eyes were closed. There were no bandages that I could see, no outward signs of violence.

She must have been a bit doped because when she opened her eyes and looked at me the fright that grew in them came very slowly. She said, "You're not one of the men—" And then she said, "Why, you're the Englishman. From the night in Berlin. You're the man Ellen said she loved."

There was a great warmth in me. I had known Ellen loved me. Just as she knew I loved her. But people live alone, all alone in the world. From birth to death they strive to mitigate that aloneness; they want most of all to let someone into their minds, their hearts—more even than they wish to enter someone else's. And the only means they have for the futile attempt is words. They succeed solely through love, but by the time they reach that state, if ever, they have become accustomed to seeking and pleading with words. And so by habit, I had needed those unnecessary words. Ellen had said them; not to me—we'd never had the time—but she had told this girl that she loved me.

It was a great warmth.

I said, "My name is John Terrant."

She said, "Of course. I remember."

There was a moment of silence as we both remembered.

As I looked at Natasha I found it easy to understand Mr. Dimitrios's and Mr. Green's enthusiasm. This Natasha, this woman, was beautiful by far more than the exotic girl I had met so briefly two years before. The long pale hair was combed straight back from her forehead and bound in braids around her head. The effect was one of simplicity, unlike the swaying, would-be seductiveness of the young Natasha. The beautiful cheekbones now looked moulded, real, part of the structure of her face; previously they had seemed glamorous but theatrical, as if she had cleverly painted them on for the evening.

I said, "What happened, Natasha?"

She said, "I did something very, very foolish. When I walked into the hotel lobby—"

I said, "No. Not then. From the beginning."

I moved forward from the door and sat in the chair beside the bed. It was, surprisingly, cooler and pleasanter in the little room than it had been at any moment since I arrived in the States. It was an illogical place and time, but I felt more nearly content, more at peace there than I had for two years.

I said, "Tell me from the beginning."

"Oh." Natasha looked bewildered and tired. "I have refused to tell the policemen anything. Not even my name. Because I don't know what's right or wrong to tell them. I don't know. But you—I'm sure it's not wrong to tell you."

I said, "It's right to tell me."

"Yes, I think, too. But then—I'm not sure what is the beginning, what place to start from." Her accent seemed even greater than it had in Berlin, but it was different in some subtle way. I couldn't quite put my finger on the change.

"The phone call I think is the beginning. So—I am a married woman, I live in Paris, where Ellen"—she paused—"where Ellen Content sent me two years ago." That probably accounted for the changed accent. "First I lived under the name she gave me. Then I got married, and now my name is real. I am Mme André Giroux."

There was great pride in her voice. She heard the echo of it and smiled at me.

"I am Mme André Giroux," she repeated, holding the smile, "and I have a little daughter, Zita—Zita was my mother's nickname—has not yet eight months. My mother died, Mr. Terrant. She could not live without Papa. But she died peacefully; she was not being stamped on by devils. Ellen saved her from that.

"So I live in Paris. My husband is a wholesale butcher. I do not dance. Not because he objects, but because my life is too full of so many other things. I have a daughter—Oh, yes. I told you that." She smiled again in apology for her pride. Then she took a deep breath, which seemed to cause her pain. She flinched, closed her eyes, finished the difficult business of the deep breath, and then went on. "So one day the phone rings. It is someone who asks if I am the same person as my maiden name, the name Ellen Content gave to my mother and me. This is mixed up, but you understand?"

I nodded.

"This woman on the phone, she speaks in Russian, and that frightens me very much. I have not speak Russian since my mother died. I stay away from the *émigrés* because Ellen Content tells us, when she sends us to France, that we must not ever see the other Russians in Paris, that that is where they will seek for us.

"But this woman on the telephone gives me a message in Russian. She tells me to learn it by heart, and she repeats it until I do. I am very careful to learn it well because she says that the message is from Ellen Content.

"Ellen Content saved my life and my mother's life, Mr. Terrant. When I tell her this that night in Berlin, and try so hard to say thank you, she say, No. It is her job. If she not do it, someone else would. And this, I think, may be the truth, but she still save my life, and Mama's life. So I listen with much attention to the long message, and I remember it most carefully.

"I am to sail on the steamship, the *Queen Elizabeth*. I am to dance in four American towns in four cafés. Everything is arranged. When I first come to New York City I am to go to the St. Regis Hotel and ask for two letters in the name of Stephanie Stetson. I was very disappointed in the St. Regis Hotel. I think maybe the letters will be from Ellen. But there are no letters. So I go to do the rest—I am to dance in four American towns in four cafés. The bookings have been arranged. Then I am to come home. This is all, but she says it will save Ellen's life.

"That is the message. The woman on the telephone will answer no questions.

"About a year ago, Mr. Terrant, I went to the American Embassy in Paris and ask for Ellen. They did not answer questions either, but something about the way of them—the *air*—made me know that although Mother and I reached Paris and lived, something happened to Ellen Content that night, or because of that night.

"So if it will save Ellen's life? I did not want to leave small Zita, and André was very afraid for me to come, but I explained to him that I had him and he had me and we had Zita only because of Ellen Content. So I came."

"And that's all?"

"That is all. I come. I am expected. I dance. These men—these Mr. Green, Mr. Dimitrios, they are innocents. That is clear. They have letters, they have pictures I did not send to them. I dance. And that is all.

"Except that I am followed. From before I first get on the ship, I am followed, everywhere, all the time. It makes me afraid, always afraid. At night on the ship, at night in the hotels, on the long train rides, I shake. I do not sleep.

"Perhaps it is because I am so tired and so afraid that I do the so foolish thing in the hotel in this city. After all, maybe Ellen wishes me to be followed, maybe that is the reason for me to take the trip. But I was frightened and I thought, Nothing is happening. I make something happen.

"I did." She closed her eyes and shuddered slightly. "I made something happen. I got shot. Just a little bit away from the heart, the doctor tells me. I was standing in front of the hotel desk and one of the men who was following me was in the lobby. I do not know how I knew it. I never really saw these followers, but I *knew* it. So beside the desk is a policeman. He is wearing a business suit, but you know how they look like a policeman just the same? All unconcerned, but no place to go and no reason to stand there?"

I smiled and nodded. I had not known until Natasha explained, but it was suddenly quite clear.

"So I quickly moved away from the desk to him and I said, 'Can you help? Someone is following me.'

"He looked as if he had been asleep and I had awakened him—but very wide awake. He said, 'Who?'

"I turned around to look, and I started to point at a group of men—I was sure the follower was among them—and as I lifted my arm, someone shot me."

There was a noise in the hospital corridor. I got up hastily and looked out. The corridor was deserted, but I could hear sounds from the stairwell. I turned back to Natasha.

"I'm trying to find Ellen, too. But I'll have to stay free to do it. So I have to get out of here. There has been a policeman posted at the door, hasn't there?"

She nodded.

"Well, he'll certainly come back at any minute. So I'll have to get out of here. But tell me quickly about the real beginning. What happened before—in Berlin?"

Natasha looked surprised. "Didn't you know? Well, there was very little to know. Papa—"

There was another noise in the corridor. I felt I was straining my luck. I interrupted: "Never mind, thanks. It will have to wait. I've really got to go."

Natasha said, "But one moment—what will I do? When I am better, what will I do?"

It was quite a question. It seemed to have no answer. I said, "Go home, Mrs. Giroux. Just go home."

She smiled tremulously. "You think I have done—"

"Well. And all you can. After all, you did what you thought Ellen asked. What maybe Ellen did ask. So go home."

I said, "Good-bye, Natasha. Be happy. Pray that I find Ellen, will you?"

She nodded. She looked very sleepy, and tears had started to fall slowly down her cheeks. I opened the door a crack. The corridor was still deserted, and I put a foot into it. Then I turned back. Natasha's eyes had closed.

I whispered, "Natasha. Natasha!"

Her lashes moved heavily upward.

"One more thing. You were to dance in four towns. What was the fourth town?"

Natasha sighed. She said, "Bing-gham-ton." And then her eyes shut tight.

14

As I look back now I realize that I must have been very near the fall-down exhaustion point. I didn't realize it then. Except for the nap I'd had in Albany I had done almost no sleeping, and certainly no relaxing. I had been sitting on trains and in buses; I had been through emotional crises and nerve shocks.

The visit to Natasha had been an intense emotional strain for me. By just existing, by lying in the little white bed and looking hopefully up at me, she had brought to reality something that had been almost a dream. I had been in pursuit, stubborn, unyielding pursuit, of Ellen, but in some subconscious fashion I had not really believed in my own determination. Ellen was a dream that I was pursuing, and in a way, I now saw dimly, some part of me had been refusing to encompass what my mind thought. To give up the belief in Ellen's existence, to accept the fact that she had been a tiny fragment of my life, a small flower in the border of the large tapestry, was to renounce happiness and its future possibility. This I had blindly, stubbornly, refused to do.

Now, however, I had looked at Natasha Paviloff Giroux, and in the looking—in the actuality, the presence of one of the participants of the Berlin experience—Ellen became real, too—possible, alive, to be found.

This rearrangement of my attitude was a bewildering experience to one so tired, and to that bewilderment I proceeded to add the physical insanity of miles and miles of walking.

I had realized, with the dying remnants of my intelligence, that police would be stationed at the railroad and bus stations. So after I picked up my suitcase, I just walked.

I have very little sense of direction, and I walked for a long time before I got out of slums, business districts, and residential areas. It occurs to me now that I may have been going in a circle. Eventually—at about one o'clock in the morning—I saw ahead of me the crossroads of a highway. And as the highway loomed ahead the fact that I was being followed was unmistakably impressed on me.

A less tired man, a man more used to such expeditions than I, must certainly have known it sooner. Indeed, I *had* known it. I had simply thrown the knowledge off as a further complication that I was too exhausted to add to my burden.

But now my mind was forced to register the fact that it was an odd kind of following. It had started soft and low, and it had become increasingly obvious until the people—not person—behind me were thrashing about.

"Thrashing" was a peculiar word for my mind to have supplied, and I realized its origin. Once, in Germany, we had been in a state of utter disorganization, and because I couldn't tell anyone else what to look for, I had gone off to do a bit of scouting myself. I had walked a considerable distance, and after that first hundred yards I had known I was being tracked, not by one German but by several. However, they couldn't have been country men, brought up as I was among woods and hills and streams, because they knew nothing about terrain, and they thrashed though the bracken on that black countryside in a way that had, in spite of the danger, been almost amusing. In the end, that night, I had found it frightfully easy to give them the slip.

But in Utica I did not seem to be trying. The men behind me were getting closer and noisier, and I was still making no effort to get away from them.

And then one of my pursuers—or I supposed he was a pursuer—ran up behind me. He made no attempt to dissemble; in fact, he called out something—I didn't catch the words, but they were obviously a cry to me to wait. I turned obediently around and waited. I put up no guard; I just stood there; heaven alone knows what I expected—I seemed to be blank of thought.

He came panting up, a thick-set, short man, and started to talk before he reached me. His speech was very hard to understand because his breathlessness was complicated by a strange accent I found difficult to place. I never did place it; it was the American accent overlying the foreign that made it so hard for me. But I finally understood some of what he was trying to say.

"Sir—none of my concern—shouldn't mix in—but do you know that you are being followed?"

I said wearily, "Why, yes. *You* are following me."

"No, no! My friend and I merely take walk. We see two men go after you, and we become curious. Then it seems to us unfair. You are alone; we think maybe you—"

At that moment, a man came up behind him, and from something in their attitude I knew this was his friend. Immediately behind *him* came two other men.

And then we just stood there, the five of us, in a tight little circle.

We had moved beyond the suburbs, and there were no street lights, but the highway lights, a hundred feet distant, sent a little illumination in our direction. Still, it was not sufficient for me to get a good look at any of the four men, and if one of them were to walk up to me at this minute I am sure I would not know him.

My self-appointed protector made the first move. At the time my mind registered the fact that it was a premature, ill-advised move that would certainly precipitate matters, but even if I had tried to undo it—and my mind was operating much too slowly to dictate such an attempt—it was too late. He reached out and pushed one of the second group and said, "What you mess in, huh?"

The man who was pushed reached, strangely enough, for me. He seemed to be trying not so much to hit me as to grab me, clasp me in some way. I avoided his grasp, set my suitcase slowly down, and as I came up from the crouch I hit him firmly on the chin. Considering my condition, it was a marvellous blow. He actually was lifted off the ground a couple of inches before he went sailing backward. I never saw where he landed, because at that moment

Protector Number Two took an awkward blow at the remaining member of the second twosome. He missed, and the man came back with a scientific defence—a quick cross punch, and then, with his arms held wide, he made for me.

And that set the pattern of the five-minute battle that followed. I stood almost passively, taking an occasional blow at the late-comers whenever the opportunity presented itself. But no one seemed inclined to do much about retaliating in kind. When one of the four got free he would clasp me in a bear hug and try to drag me bodily away, and the other faction would immediately set me free.

The brawl was almost silent, except for one man who kept saying, "Now, look—Now, look—" in unaccented English. I never distinguished who the conversationalist was.

After five minutes, I saw an unprotected chin, hit out at it, connected, not too powerfully, and then realized that the recipient had been one of my protectors. Or so I thought. And that decided me. The whole thing was much too confused for me. I was too weary for this bewildering, inchoate nonsense, I didn't know what the stakes were, and I simply resigned from it.

I picked up my luggage—the mêlée had moved a few yards from it—and I walked, not too quickly, to the highway, and looked around. At that junction there were a number of signs pointing to towns and giving directions, but the only one that registered in my fumbling mind was a round one that said "N. Y. State—5S."

I put my suitcase down—it had grown very heavy—and looked back. I could hear the sounds of battle, but I couldn't distinguish any forms in the blackness. Apparently they had not yet discovered that I was no longer a participant, because although I couldn't see them, they could easily have seen me as I stood on the edge of the lighted highway.

While I was twisted away from the road, looking into the darkness behind me, there was a roar and a squeal, and as I turned to face it I saw that an enormous lorry had pulled up in front of me. There were two men in the front, and the one nearest leaned down and yelled over the lorry's roar, "Wanna lift?"

I nodded. He opened the door, and I climbed the steep step and sat beside him.

The roar increased as the driver shifted gears, and then we moved off along the straight, well-lighted road.

The noise didn't deter the driver from trying to make conversation. "We're not supposed to pick up people," he bellowed, "but it seems pretty safe when there's two of us. Take quite a guy to get both of us!" He laughed uproariously.

I turned my head towards him, and I saw what he meant. They were very large, burly men. Still, I suppose the comment was intended as a warning.

The driver yelled, "Ought to make good time tonight. It's hot, but in one way the heat kinda pays off. Everybody stays home, turns on the fan, and drinks beer. This isn't the fastest crate in the world, but with no traffic like this I bet we get in by seven."

I clamped my hand along my jawbone and yelled back, "Where are you going?"

There was a small pause. Then the man in the middle said, as quietly as possible over the roar, "We're going to New York. Where're *you* going?"

The implication was clear: they didn't care much for people who had no explicit destination. It was a sensible way of reasoning, now that I think it over. I said hastily, "Oh, I'm hoping to reach New York. What I meant is, *how* are you going?"

It was the right question. The driver launched enthusiastically into a discussion of the merit of Route 5 as opposed to Route 5S. "Usually, in Alexandra, I branch off on to Five—What's a matter, Mac? You got a toothache?"

"Killin' muh."

"Ah, now, that's a shame."

Before he had finished the sentence, a sickly blue neon light loomed ahead, and the driver, evidently a man of impulse, instantly applied his brakes. The big lorry stopped in racking agony in front of an all-night restaurant. "Frank," he shouted—apparently his occupational voice had become habitual—"go in and bring him some aspirin."

My mumbled protests did no good. I got out of the cab, and Frank went sulkily off towards the blue lights while my guardian guided me to the back of the lorry.

"Guess what we're trucking? Naw, you'd never guess. Well, it's mattresses, see?" He laughed heartily. "They're all crated up, but Frank and me are no dopes. Over there, back there in the right corner, is one we've got kinda loose"—the "kinda loose" mattress was frankly exposed—"and you're gonna lie down on that. Here"—Frank was at his elbow with a paper cup and some loose pills—"take these and lie down and try and relax. That'll do it."

I swallowed the pills and crawled into the lorry, lugging the heavy suitcase. Under the driver's stern eye I collapsed on the mattress. In a minute the lorry rumbled off.

It should have been hot in the back of the lorry, but there was a wonderful gale blowing through from somewhere. The mattress was soft, the aspirins were an unusual indulgence, the roar was muted. . . .

15

MANHATTAN ISLAND, although preparing to steam, was still comparatively cool at seven-thirty in the morning.

The driver, who was just as happy by light of day but seemed even bigger, refused ten dollars, looking quite hurt, and put me down at the corner of Forty-Second Street and Second Avenue. He explained that if I walked two blocks to the west I would be back at the hotel I named—the one I had briefly stayed at when I landed.

And so, just a couple of days after that landing, I found myself again high above the streets of New York in one of the anonymous rooms of the enormous hotel. By eight-thirty I had done all the things I had not had time for—showered, shaved, sent shirts to be washed and suit to be pressed—and I was sitting in my room over an enormous breakfast.

I think my activity and bustle was a diversionary tactic, an attempt to avoid thinking, to feel physically organized and clear of clutter, because a next step was indicated and I had no least idea of what it should be.

But by eight-thirty breakfast was almost over and my excuses gone. I *had* to think.

I spent a few minutes looking moodily down on the tiny roofs of the cars below me and thinking fuzzily of the serio-comic street battle of the night before. But the fuzziness wouldn't pass: I didn't know who the participants were; I didn't know what they had wanted. I had got clear. That would have to suffice for the minute.

My next step. What should I do now? Should I go to Binghamton? There was my map with its three crosses. I added the fourth. Binghamton, Natasha had said, was the last stop. What would I find in Binghamton? Another night club, another Mr. Dimitrios—a disappointed one—and what else? Natasha had absolved the night-club owners of any knowledge of what was going on, and I agreed with her.

So going to Binghamton seemed, on the face of it, profitless.

And then my next step arose and stared at me.

I had had no opportunity to follow up the cab driver's statement that Natasha had stopped at the St. Regis hotel. But now I was not only near by; I had, in addition, the further knowledge, from Natasha, that a Stephanie Stetson was somehow involved.

The St. Regis, then. I folded my maps, put them in the bureau drawer, and left the room.

The St. Regis Hotel was perhaps a quarter of an hour's walk from my hotel—and a twenty-minute cab drive. In the cab I discovered—in the brief time I dared take my eyes off the traffic—that in the business of changing suits I had left all my papers and identification in the bureau drawer. I had a notecase with me, so it didn't really matter.

The chauffeur, as evidenced by the way in which he drove, was insane. The more clearly so since no amount of steeplechase driving could possibly hurdle the traffic or in any way shorten the time of the trip. I reached the St. Regis alive, but shaken.

There was something rather British about the interior of the hotel. It was not all newly varnished, it was not modem in *décor,* and its leisurely pace contrasted delightfully with the breakneck ride I had just escaped from. And before the desk clerk opened his mouth, I knew he was a fellow countryman.

I was careful to word my request in the exact fashion in which Natasha had passed it on to me. Perhaps I had some silly notion that this enormous and distinguished hostelry was involved in a game of passwords and intrigue. 'Have you two letters in the name of Stephanie Stetson?' I asked.

Perhaps if the clerk had not been a compatriot I could not have read his exasperation so clearly, for all he said was, "No, sir. We have not." But he said it with vast distinctness, and he did not make the usual check through the stack of unassigned mail.

I said, "Oh."

There was an arid pause. He examined me politely enough, but with the obvious intention of volunteering nothing.

I pushed on: "Well, did Miss Stetson ever stop here?"

"No, sir."

"I see. . . . May I ask how you know there is no mail for Miss Stetson without checking to make certain?"

He took a deep breath. "Because, sir, I have looked twice this week, both times for—foreigners. If any mail had arrived since the last time I looked it would have made an—an indelible impression on me. The last—gentleman—was extremely violent about the request." Distaste was clear on his face. I wondered briefly if he appreciated the humour of his terminology. But then I realized that his definition of "foreigners" undoubtedly encompassed all people who did not speak unaccented English, even when they were resident in their own countries.

I said, "Thank you." There was nothing to be gained.

I walked down the few steps, strolled to the corner, and moved slowly down Fifth Avenue.

Two people had asked for the letters. Did anyone get them? No. No, that was easily followed through. The first person who asked was Natasha. She had not got the letters. I could hear her tired voice saying, "I was very disappointed in the St. Regis Hotel. . . ." So the second applicant, a man and a foreigner, must have been one of her pursuers. And he would not have been "violent" if his request had been granted.

I tried to put myself in the position of my predecessor, the violent foreigner. Like me, he had been refused at the desk of the St. Regis, he had left the lobby, walked down the few steps, and walked or ridden away. What would he have done then?

Tried to find Stephanie Stetson, presumably.

But how?

Stephanie Stetson—a strangely alliterative name. Unusual enough, in fact—I quickened my pace—so that there would not be many who bore it. I might not have had the experience for my mission, but I *was* helped by that very lack. A kind of simplicity, an inevitability of direction, moved me from step to step.

A policeman directing traffic at an intersection told me patronizingly where to find a telephone booth. I went, as instructed, into one of the tall buildings lining the street, and was directed and redirected along yards of corridors. But when I came to the booths I shunned them for the telephone books.

A Stephanie Stetson lived in Manhattan, on Eighth Street.

There was no one by that name in any of the other books.

I sat down in one of the empty booths and thought it over. Should I telephone? I decided against it. I wanted to see Miss Stetson. If she was at home she might be forewarned—against what, I did not know, but it seemed better to take her by surprise, if possible. If she was not at home that knowledge would put me no for'arder, since I would nevertheless go to her home and await her return.

I would go to Eighth Street.

16

THE taxi drivers were all cut of the same cloth. I arrived at the Eighth Street address breathless and full of information. Among that information was the fact that I was now in Greenwich Village, and a crooked and dilapidated section it was.

The street on which Miss Stetson lived was quiet, shabby, and rather more respectable-looking than the neighbouring squares. Her house, a small block of flats, was a dingy grey stone. Inside there were two vertical rows of bells, each with a name beside it. Stephanie Stetson lived in 3R; "R" seemed to stand for "rear."

I pressed the button and waited. The door, I decided, was controlled from the apartments, where the residents could press a buzzer, thus disengaging the main-door lock.

But nothing happened. Miss Stetson was, it seemed, not at home.

I walked down the street. Then I walked back. I stood on the corner and tried to plan. Stand around indefinitely? Go away and come back? Leave a note asking her to call my hotel? No; not the last. I was stubbornly and blindly determined to give the lady no opportunity to anticipate my visit.

I walked back to the house and pressed the bell again. It was a silly gesture; not a living soul had passed me as I patrolled the street. Of course there was no answer.

I leaned against the pseudo-marble wall and contemplated the door. The house was very badly tended; the door-bell might very well not work, or if it did, perhaps the mechanism that disengaged the lock was out of repair; on the other hand, the door's lock might not be in working order, either.

It wasn't.

I mounted two flights of stairs and almost climbed the third before I recalled that the Americans number their storeys differently from the way we do—what I call the second storey would be their third.

As I had suspected, it was the door at the rear that was marked "3R." In further substantiation there was a neat, printed card—"Mlle Stephanie Stetson." Stetson seemed very un-French to me, but that was of small matter.

There was a minute brass knocker, but no one answered my prolonged series of knocks.

I stared futilely at the peeling paint on the door for a few minutes, and then I moved to the window flanking Number 3R and transferred my stare to the blank brick wall which backed up on the flats and apparently represented the rear view.

My next move came only after a great deal of inner turmoil. We English are extremely conscious of property rights. It is my impression—I may be wrong, of course—but I believe that we treat the invasion of a person's home more seriously than do Americans.

So I thought it out very carefully. Then I went and tried Miss Stetson's door.

It was locked.

I returned to the window, and watched the sun try to crowd down the area-way.

It had slowly begun to seem to me that Miss Stetson's absence might be considered as a stroke of good luck. Since I had no idea of the degree of her involvement in the business, talking to her *after* I knew something about her might produce better results. . . . Her home *might* yield a clue—or, at least, a hint. . . .

The hall window was on a fire escape, a solid-looking iron structure. I leaned out of the opened window and looked to my right. The fire escape terminated at the window of a room which was undoubtedly in Miss Stetson's apartment. In view of the terrible heat, it was not surprising that it was open. To my left there was a slit-like view of the street. It looked deserted.

There was nothing dangerous or acrobatic about the venture. I simply got my longish legs out of the corridor window, took three or four steps, and slid in through Miss Stetson's window. Nevertheless, as I stood still inside the small room I was, unaccountably, shaking.

I was in a kitchen, a small old-fashioned kitchen, quite unlike the gleaming, spick-and-span affairs the American magazines would lead one to believe are prevalent in their country. The room was neither dirty nor clean; in general, it was free of clutter, but there were some eggish-looking dishes in the sink on my left and an inexplicable pool of water beneath my feet. I moved away from the window out of the puddle and went straight ahead into a short, wide, foyer-like hallway.

The plan of the flat was very simple. To my right was a door; that, its appearance and my sense of direction told me, was the main entrance. Opposite me was a door that stood slightly ajar; to the left was a closed door; and at the left end of the little hallway was an open archway through which I could see a cluttered drawing-room that seemed to be dominated by an amazingly large grand piano. I moved quietly towards the drawing-room, stopping *en route* to verify my suspicion that the door on the left led into a cupboard.

On the other side of the arch was a big, extremely high-ceilinged room that must once have been a pleasant place. It had six windows, four at the rear, two facing the areaway on which the kitchen looked out. But since the house was erected, I should imagine forty or so years before, the great brick expanse had gone up in the next street— it looked as if it might be a theatre, possibly a cinema—and one could now touch that blank wall from any of the rear four windows without leaning dangerously far out. As a result there was, even on a bright sunshiny day like the present one, almost no light in the big room. This circumstance reduced the shabby furnishings to an even dingier appearance than they deserved.

The room was overfurnished, cluttered. In addition to the massive piano, there were four vast, overstuffed chairs covered in printed materials so faded that their original patterns were now merely hinted at. There was one large divan and one smaller one. There was a mantelpiece crowded, heaped—almost overwhelmed—by photographs. I moved towards it—I discovered I was tiptoeing—and my heart gave a terrific lurch as someone moved towards me. In the next instant I felt consummately foolish as I realized I had caught a glimpse of myself in the dusty mirror that topped the fireplace and moved stretchingly upward to the distant ceiling.

The photographs cleared up the use of the word "Mademoiselle" on the door. The French form of address is often affected by singers, and Mademoiselle was a singer. There were pictures of her bedecked in costume for every soprano role I had ever heard of, and the inscriptions ranged over the entire operatic world. None of them showed a woman of over thirty-five, but, from the hair styles, the stiffness of the poses, the ineptness of the photography, and a general air of age about them, I judged that Mademoiselle was now well past middle age.

Altogether she was a surprise to me. I think I had had an unacknowledged hope that, for some reason no less inexplicable than the rest of my experiences, Stephanie Stetson would turn out to be Ellen.

Well, she would not. But, and I considered myself quite foolish for the conviction but could not shake it off, neither was she a villainess in the piece.

Stephanie's face in the old photographs was most unsoprano-like in that it was invariably sweet. She was pretty, although even in those pictures which had been taken when she was no more than twenty-eight or so, hers showed as a fading kind of prettiness. But most of all she was gentle and kind-looking.

If Stephanie could, she would help, not hinder me.

The conviction decided me: I would get out of there immediately, leave a note under the entrance door, as if inserted from the outside, and return to my hotel to await her telephone call. I felt increasingly shabby at my invasion of the lady's home.

I hesitated at the immense piano, and then took up a green, leather-bound book that lay prominently on its surface. I blew the dust off—the apartment was exceedingly dusty—and opened it. The contents of the book, which showed a series of appointments at half-hour intervals, added to the sheet music spread on the piano rack, which ran from marked bass parts to lyric soprano, told of Miss Stetson's present means of livelihood: she taught singing.

I put the book down carefully in its dust-free former position and walked firmly down the hall towards the front door; I felt that I had done quite enough prying.

As I passed the door, now on my left, opposite the kitchen, I confirmed my guess that it led to the bedroom. I could see the foot of a bed covered by a rose-coloured counterpane, and beyond that a door opened into what must have been a bathroom. I continued down the short hall, put my hand on the entrance door's knob, and paused.

I had an eerie feeling. Something . . . What was the matter? And then I knew.

Something had moved in that bathroom.

I stood painfully still; one of my feet was only half on the ground and I forbore to put it all the way down. And then I realized that my frozen silence was ridiculous. Whoever or whatever was in that bathroom knew that I was in the apartment. I had been quiet, yes. But by no means silent.

Whoever or whatever . . . Perhaps that was the answer. Perhaps it was a cat or a dog. But a dog would have barked, and all cats are nosy Parkers.

I realized then that I was frightened, and it made me curiously angry. I had been frightened before in my life, of course; during a war men live in periods of peace between periods of fright. But in this case it was so formless. . . .

I took a deep breath, put my foot firmly on the floor, took my hand off the door-knob, and tried to breathe evenly. What had I seen that made me so sure there was a movement? The memory came, it escaped me, and then it came back. I had seen a shadow. Something beyond my field of vision had moved, and it had cast a shadow. Well, if a window were open, and a curtain had billowed . . .

I couldn't possibly walk out of the flat—I should be eternally ashamed. So I went up the hall and through the bedroom and into the small bathroom.

My surmise had been correct. A small window was open, the air was drifting gently in, and the fluttery draperies in which Mademoiselle Stetson was dressed were moving gently to and fro as she hung from the shower rod.

17

My first instinct was to cut her down; my second was to get out of there. I fought between the two, and then for a minute nausea added itself to the struggle.

I went back into the bedroom and sat heavily on the rose counterpane. Couldn't cut her down: police would object; no use to it, anyway. Miss Stetson was dead, irrevocably and thoroughly. A war had taught me . . . But in war I hadn't seen people who had been hanged. Certainly not old ladies whose faces . . .

I tried to get myself in hand, but it was difficult. Until that moment I had been involved, or had been trying to involve myself, in a shapeless, misty series of events. Ed Bigeby had died, it was true. But I hadn't seen him die; there was always a remote chance that it *had* been just a brawl.

I was undergoing an experience similar to that which I had suffered on the previous evening. The sight of Natasha had given immediacy and reality to the problem; the sight of Miss Stetson gave immediacy and reality to its horror, its danger. Ellen's danger. My danger. Ed's danger. Miss Stetson's—

Well, I could no longer go dashing about alone. I had ignored the request of Mr. Eider, the command of Divisional Superintendent Jelliffson, the rights of the Utica police. But this was cold-blooded murder, and I am really a law-abiding citizen.

It *was* murder, I knew, because the shower rod was not high and Miss Stetson's feet dangled into the bathtub. No one can successfully hang himself when there is a permanent footrest immediately beneath him. And the flat edge of the bathtub was a very permanent footrest that Miss Stetson could not have avoided.

She had been, *must* have been, rendered unconscious before she was hanged.

The old civilian contention that a policeman is never at hand when you need him held true. I should have telephoned, of course—the phone was right there beside the bed—but I simply never thought of it. I went out of the door, and down the stairs, and then I walked. I not only don't know how far I walked, I don't even know where I walked. I went down one street and then, faced by a triangle, I chose a side of it. At the next intersection I turned right because the street looked busier; the street of my choice prescribed a circle, or perhaps just an oval.

I eventually saw a policeman ahead, and then I had to chase him for a block before I could catch up with him. I said, "I say!" twice before he slowly turned around. Then when I was face to face with him, my heart sank. He was visibly ponderous of body and obviously ponderous of mind. But there was nothing for it. I said, "I've just found a dead woman. Murdered. Will you come?"

He stared at me. "Where?"

I waved to my right. Then I reconsidered the gesture and flapped my hand off to the left. Then I paused and said, on a rising note: "Eighth Street."

"Where on Eighth?"

I told him the number.

He stared dubiously at me. "Looks like you don't know where you been. Are you sure you know what you seen? That number's *that* way." He pointed directly in front of us.

Well, it was possible. I had certainly made at least one circle. "No matter," I said. "The important thing is that she is dead. Will you come and let me show you?"

He lifted the back of his jacket, exposing an enormous gun and an even more enormous behind. From a pocket in this tremendous area he produced a tiny notebook. He laboriously extracted a pencil, opened the book, and asked, "What's your name?"

"What's the difference? John Terrant. Will you—"

"T-u-r—"

"T-e-double-r-a-n-t."

"What was that address?"

I told him.

"Is that your address?"

"No."

"Well, what is your address and how did you come to discover the body?"

"Look," I said, "don't you think you could ask these questions later?"

He raised his eyes from the notebook. "Why? You said she's dead, didn't you?"

There was impeccable logic in his point of view. Or was there? "Well," I said slowly, with a carefully fraudulent implication, "of course I'm not a physician. . . ."

I could see the thought seep through—not quickly, but it got there. "Okay," he said, "C'mon."

Sometime during his life he had established a pace, and he held to it in spite of murder. At the corner he stopped, went to a box hanging on a pole, and opened it to expose a telephone. From the ensuing conversation I gathered that it was a direct line to the police station.

He said, "Morgan. Got a guy in tow"—it seemed to me a most dubious explanation of who had whom—"who reports a murder. . . . Yeah. On Eighth." He gave the number. "He *said* murder. . . . Dunno. . . . Yeah. . . . Yeah. Okay."

He hung up. And we crept onward.

Miss Stetson's building was only two blocks away, although I had walked at least five. We approached it from the opposite side. As we neared the building a small green and white coupé with a search-light on its hood drew in from the other end of the street. It pulled up to the kerb in front of Miss Stetson's house, and two uniformed policemen got out. My escort left me and joined them. After they had held a muttered, seemingly desultory consultation on the pavement, one of the newcomers turned to me and said, "Okay, buddy, this it?"

"Yes. If you'll follow me—"

"All right. Go ahead."

With me in the lead we marched in single file through the dingy, would-be-marble passage, past the push buttons, through the main door, and up two flights of stairs.

I said, "That's the door leading into her rooms"—one of the men brushed past me and grabbed the knob—"but it's locked. We have to go in this way." I swung my legs through the window. As I stood erect on the steel slats I caught a glimpse of one of the new policemen; he looked entirely nonplussed.

I said, "Do come along." He did.

When we had gained the kitchen, I turned around and asked, "Where are the others?"

He examined me curiously. "Any good reason we can't just let 'em in the front door?" He stepped out of the puddle of water, brushed past me, and opened the entrance door. I noticed that he carefully covered his hand with a handkerchief before he touched the knob.

I waved the three men through the bedroom towards the bath, but I didn't follow. I couldn't possibly have looked at Miss Stetson again.

They didn't cross the bathroom's threshold either—I doubt if the room would have held them—but they clustered in the doorway. The man who had followed me over the fire escape—he seemed to have taken command—said "God!" Then he turned around and came over to where I stood, half in the hall and half in the bedroom.

"Okay," he said, with a kind of acceptance. I wondered at it. Did the residents of New York City habitually report murders that hadn't taken place?

He added, "Let's see the rest of the place."

He took me by the elbow as we moved into the hall. It was a peculiar gesture, and it made me suddenly and acutely uncomfortable. But there seemed no way, without indulging in the petulant shrug of a four-year-old, to rid myself of the grasp.

The tour naturally didn't take half a minute. Like me, he opened the cupboard door and then moved through the archway. He stared around the room for a minute and then said again, "Okay." He piloted me to a chair near the arch. "You sit there."

I sat down in the big chair, and he started out of the room. But before he reached the arch he turned around and addressed me again: "Don't touch anything—not a *thing*. There'll be no danger of forgetting if you just don't get out of that chair."

18

I SPENT an hour and forty-five minutes in that room. After the first few minutes the policeman I had flagged on the street came and sat opposite me. I think he was, by nature, incapable of conversation, and he seemed entirely happy just to be off his feet. After a bit I realized that I didn't mind it very much either. The sight of Miss Stetson's body swinging in the gentle breeze had been a considerable shock to me; the silence was therapy.

Fifteen minutes after I had been deposited in the chair, a squat, powerful-looking, red-faced man in brown—brown suit, hat, shoes, *and* tie, came in and looked at me. His was a dead stare, not curious, not inimical, but rather preoccupied. Just as I was beginning to feel like a specimen of something strange, he said, "Your name is Terrant?" And to my nod, "Well, we'll be going in a few minutes." He started out of the room. I said, "And what's your name?"

He looked surprised by the question. Then he said, "Oh, I'm Kelly. I am Lieutenant Kelly." And then he repeated, "We'll be going in a few minutes."

Well, we went an hour and a half later. Kelly and I and the astounding number of men who had collected in the small flat—some in civilian dress, some in uniform—poured out of the flat and down the stairs, past the curious faces that hung out of the doors that had been mute, closed surfaces when I first entered the building.

The street, too, had come alive. What had been a somnolent, curiously empty by-way a few hours before now was crowded by three patrol coupés, two saloons, and what I at first mistook for an ambulance, and the pavement was choked by gawkers.

I was ushered into one of the waiting saloon cars, and Kelly and one of his anonymous fellow workers joined me in the back seat. A third man climbed in beside the driver.

Ten minutes later we left the car, walked up a few steps, and into an institutional-looking building.

Kelly led me through dirty grey halls and into a small room, where he waved me into a chair opposite a desk. He went around and sat himself behind the desk. Two other men entered and sat behind me.

It was unbearably hot in the little room.

Kelly looked down at the desk's surface, but he seemed to be addressing me. He said, "Sorry to have kept you waiting." The words were entirely perfunctory; he wasn't in the least sorry. "But now we've finished with the preliminary routine, so let's get to it."

He waited, his eyes on the desk.

Something was apparently expected of me. I finally said, "Get to it?"

His heavy eyelids flicked up—everything about him was heavy—and he said impatiently, "Your story, Mr. Terrant; your story, please."

"Oh." My brain belatedly awakened to the need for collecting itself, and my thoughts went scurrying furiously along, but one would never have known that if the words I produced were to have been taken as evidence. I said, "Well, she didn't answer the door, so I went in through the window and found her."

There was a moment's silence, and then Kelly said, "I see." The words were unaccented, but his expression, which until then had been one of irritated boredom, was giving way to a kind of clinical interest. "Let's start just a *little* further back. Your name is John Terrant. English?"

"Yes."

"Your address?"

"My temporary address?"

He stared at me. He said, "Well, I don't care where in England you hang your hat."

"Well, here—I'm registered at a hotel."

"*What* hotel?"

I told him.

"How long you been there?"

"I registered this morning."

He ran stubby fingers through his sandy, receding hair—it had fallen out at the temples, leaving an exaggerated peak at the centre that made him look, despite the lack of moulding in his heavy features, like an incongruously fat and irascible Mephistopheles.

He said irritably, "Now, look: I'm a busy man. I haven't time for this—this horsing around. Are you stalling, or don't you understand English? I want to know who you are. Where do you come from? What's your business? Where do you *live?*"

I opened my mouth, and then I shut it again. The explanation wasn't simple. What *was* my business of the moment? Did I start the story in the Berlin of 1948? Or did I start with the day before? Suppose I said, "I was in Utica, New York, yesterday."—And then had to explain that I wasn't registered in that hotel for even half a day. If I had told him that much, the Utica police would have plenty to add. Well, I could let them add it; after all, no one was going to suspect me of murder, or of the shooting of Natasha. Natasha would testify that I didn't shoot her. Besides, I could prove I wasn't in Utica at the time she was shot. I could probably prove I wasn't around when Miss Stetson was killed. But—

The flat of Kelly's hand came down on the desk with a crash. "Well, *well?*" His head was thrust at me in such an exaggerated fashion that he was almost lying on the desk.

I didn't jump, and I kept my face expressionless. I just went on thinking at an accelerated pace. Logically, I should explain that I had arrived in America on Tuesday and give him my London address and newspaper affiliations, but—Something about his belligerence reminded me of Jelliffson. An intelligent explanation to Kelly, and I would have Jelliffson on my hands. The British Embassy would pop up; I would be ushered on to a plane or ship . . .

And there would go my chance to find Ellen.

My voice sounded very stiff: "My name is John Terrant. I am a—novelist. I've been travelling about your country for—for some time. Rather aimlessly. In search of—of suitable material."

"I *see*." The words were heavily sarcastic. "And I suppose that clears everything up?"

I didn't answer.

"All right. Dump your pockets."

"Dump—?"

He tapped a finger on the scarred surface of the desk and spoke with insulting distinctness, as if to a wayward child. "Put everything you have in your pockets on this desk."

"Oh. Certainly." I proceeded to empty my pockets. "But"—for the first time, the situation held a little humour for me—"I'm afraid you are not going to find this material very helpful. All I have"—I named the items as I placed them on the desk's surface—"are two handkerchiefs, a notecase, loose change, and some very anonymous keys that I forgot to leave—at home."

He picked up the notecase and flicked through it. All it offered for his inspection was the remnants of the money the young man had given me on the dock. Kelly said violently, "What kind of a wallet is this? What—"

"It isn't a wallet, Lieutenant. It's a notecase. My wallet is always so crowded with papers—identification cards, notes, and so forth—that I don't attempt to carry money in it."

"It's *crowded* with identification—" He was turning quite red in the face. "And where is that bulging little item just now?"

I shrugged.

His red colour didn't abate, but he surprised me by changing the subject. "Tell me," he said, with a sarcastic show of interest, "how are you going to fit Stephanie Stetson into the meatless little story you just outlined?"

"I met her on a ship. Some time ago. She asked me to come and visit her—I'm interested in music. So—I was in New York. . . ." I trailed off. I thought it was pretty bad, but I wanted time. If I could think it out for a bit—

"And when you got there she wasn't home?"

"That's correct."

"So you went through the window. You always go through windows when your friends don't answer their door-bells?"

"No. I had a—a premonition."

His heavy face was returning to its normal lighter red colour. "You know," he said coldly, "this stuff isn't even interesting. But it is insulting to my intelligence."

I said, "I can probably prove—through the waiter who brought breakfast to my room, the desk clerk who gave me directions, the doorman who got me the cab—"

"You're talking about this morning?"

I nodded.

"You don't know that the Stetson woman was killed approximately three days ago?"

"Why, no," I said slowly. Where had I been three days before? New York? Albany—?

"Well, that wasn't very smart of you. Even if you didn't know a thing about this murder, didn't you see the colour of the woman's face?" My stomach turned over. I had, indeed, and had thought of something else as quickly as possible. "Didn't you see the dust on everything?" I opened my mouth, and he said quickly, "All right, all right. So you thought she wasn't a very good housekeeper. I can foresee that one. But what about the pool on the kitchen floor? Did you think it was for swimming? Do people usually let the rain in and then avoid the kitchen sink for over two days rather than step in the water? Because it's over two days since it rained, you know."

I didn't know, but I *should* have figured out the cause of that puddle of water. I told him the truth: "I'm simply not accustomed to murder, Lieutenant. I don't think in your terms."

"No? I understood you to say that you had a premonition. What terms were you thinking in then?"

I said doggedly, "Illness. I thought perhaps the old lady had had a heart attack or—something."

"Really? Because she was so old, huh?"

Something warned me to be quiet.

"How old are you?" he asked abruptly.

"Thirty-four."

"Um. Well, to an American of thirty-four, fifty-four doesn't seem like doddering old age. Perhaps you people are younger. The lady was fifty-four, Terrant. A healthy fifty-four, according to her doctor."

He pushed himself back in his chair and looked at me with interest. "So you didn't know Stephanie Stetson. A complete stranger?"

I didn't answer.

"—And yet you went through that window. You know," he said musingly, "even though you are a—an odd and elegant fish, an hour ago I would have said you were a nephew, the son of a friend, or maybe a pupil of the Stetson woman's. I'd have said you had been telephoning her for a couple of days, she didn't answer, that was unusual, and so you went over to see what was up. If you'd bolstered it by giving me an address and a checkable means of livelihood, that would have been a very believable story. Because there was something about the way you ran out in the street to get a cop, instead of telephoning, that struck me as being just the kind of silly thing that someone does who is taken completely by surprise."

He stood up. The boredom had returned to his face and voice. "And I still believe it. But I've added a chapter. You're wanted, I'll bet this year's salary—although that isn't much—for con or fancy signatures—some Dapper Dan operation. And this murder is probably tied in somewhere along the line."

"Well—" He dismissed me from his considerations. "Take his prints, Kolski," he said to one of the men behind me. "And you"— to the other—"go over to his hotel room. *If* he's registered there, go through his stuff and see what you can find. Then—"

I said, "Just a minute, Lieutenant."

"What?" His eyes flickered impatiently back to me.

"I would appreciate it if you would give me a minute to think before you take any precipitate steps."

"Now *would* you? You are always polite, aren't you?"

"I find it costs me very little. May I have the minute?"

I expected him to turn red in the face again and bellow, but, surprisingly, he said calmly, "Certainly," and he sat down, slouched back, and elaborately folded his hands across his thick middle.

I ignored him. All I could see before me was Jelliffson, politer than Kelly, but more telling; colder than Kelly, but more succinct; and, it seemed to me, far more powerful. Jelliffson represented the termination of my efforts to find Ellen. The hotel room's contents would lead Kelly to the New York office of the paper, and the route from there was fairly clear.

One way or another I was going to be in trouble, but as matters stood I preferred to have my trouble in America, near Natasha, if possible.

I said firmly, "I think it will save you a good deal of fuss if you will advise the Utica, New York, police that you have the Englishman who appeared at the desk of the Utica Hotel last evening at about nine o'clock."

He asked, with incomprehensible amusement, "You're wanted in Utica?"

"You find that amusing?"

"Well, it seems pretty small-town for you. What's the rap?"

"That is all I am going to say."

"You know," he said, "I believe you."

19

At four o'clock someone brought me a sandwich and a small bottle of milk. I was exceedingly grateful. Even after I understood that I was to pay for it, I was grateful.

From four o'clock until the two men arrived at nine I just sat. It was my day for sitting. But I no longer found it pleasant or relaxing. My fingerprints were taken—a messy business that I remembered having gone through in the army. Otherwise the boredom was unrelieved. I felt that I should be thinking, planning, deducing. But the heat and my nervous anticipation as to what would happen next combined to rob me of any possible success in the realm of clear thinking. Miss Stetson's death was an enigma that I had no key to. She herself and her death seemed totally unrelated to the rest of the events.

And there I stuck until, shortly after nine, the door opened and Kelly came in with two youngish men.

Kelly's face wore a rather odd expression; he looked intrigued, if that word doesn't imply a subtlety beyond Kelly's facial possibilities. He said, "Well, my dear Mr. Terrant, you are no longer to grace our offices. These gentlemen are from the FBI, and they are taking you away from us. You will be required to testify at the inquest in about a week. If we have any questions before then we'll be in touch with you. Meanwhile these gentlemen seem eager to vouch for you—or, at least, to get you." He paused, and then he smiled curiously. "It seems, Mr. Terrant, that I was right; you are not so small-town, after all."

I wasn't interested in Lieutenant Kelly's amusement. I stared at the two men who stood behind him, their hats in their hands. They were subdued-looking, my age or a trifle younger, quietly dressed, of average height, with some of the same anonymous quality I had noticed in myself.

I said, not too brilliantly, "The Federal Bureau of Investigation?"

One of them, a fairish, rather good-looking man, said, "My name is William Springer, Mr. Terrant. This is Mr. Kennedy."

"How do you do? But I thought the Utica police—"

Springer said, "We—that is, the FBI—were in Utica when you—when you were there."

"Oh, but—"

He interrupted quickly, "Let's get along now, Mr. Terrant. We can talk later."

We didn't "get along" as rapidly as Springer and Kennedy would obviously have preferred. There was a great deal of signing and conversation first. But eventually we reached the hot night air, where Springer hailed a taxi.

The three of us crawled into the cab and Springer directed the driver to my hotel.

It didn't seem right to me.

I said tentatively, "That's the hotel I'm registered at—"

Springer said, "Yes. It's pretty late and you must be tired. Better get a night's sleep."

It didn't ring true. A murder in New York. A shooting in Utica. A situation so serious that Jelliffson had shown that more than one country kept files on it. And the Federal Bureau of Investigation, which corresponded roughly to a wedding of the British Secret Service and the Special Branch of Scotland Yard, was worrying about my sleep?

Alarm grew in me—slowly but insistently. They had spirited me out of the hands of the police, it was true. The police certainly should have known if they were not bona fide members of the Federal Bureau of Investigation. But Kelly had not seemed to know them personally—or, at least, I had not got that impression. Memories of some of the daring impersonations of fact and fiction crowded in on me. Perhaps if one knew the routine involved in getting prisoners released in one's custody it would not be too difficult—

We had reached the hotel. Kennedy got out and turned towards me.

I didn't budge.

Springer, hemmed in on my left, said, "Mr. Terrant—?"

I said, "I really have no proof that you are members of the Federal Bureau of Investigation."

Springer was a very self-possessed young man, but he seemed taken aback. He said, "Oh. Well. Yes. Well, here." He reached into his pocket and brought out a small leather folder, which he flipped open and held out towards me. I leaned forward to get light from the taxi meter, and examined it. But the leather packet served only to confirm a suspicion I'd always had about identification cloak-and-dagger people carry: it meant nothing to me. It said "William Springer"; it said "Federal Bureau of Investigation"; and it contained a picture of the young man. But it didn't prove a thing.

I said, "And so?"

There was a little pause, and then Mr. Springer laughed. He said, "The American idiom, Mr. Terrant, is 'So what?'"

"Well, I don't intend to be rude, but I really don't see what that"—I waved at the leather case—"proves. I see no reason to believe in it."

Springer didn't look offended. He looked impassive and thoughtful. He said, "Commendably cautious. Now, let's see. . . . Well, we could go into the lobby, and you could telephone the office." He added hastily, "Having looked up the number in the telephone book yourself, of course."

Mr. Kennedy, a homely, pleasant-looking man, was leaning against the taxi's doorjamb. He spoke for the first time in my hearing. "I think we can convince Mr. Terrant," he said quietly. "Suppose we tell you the name of the man who called on you in London a year or so ago? His name was Luke Benjamin."

Yes. Yes, he was right; that did it. It was the kind of thing no one not in authority would know—

Kennedy added, "And the man you spoke to just before you left Berlin was Clarence Russell. Clare is about five feet eight, thin, blond. He has—"

I said, "All right, gentlemen."

Inside the hotel, Kennedy guided me towards the row of lifts, and Springer made for the hotel desk. After two or three minutes Springer joined us and the three of us silently boarded the lift.

Not a word was spoken as we proceeded upstairs and along the heavily carpeted corridor. Springer unlocked and pushed open the door to the room I had left that morning—it seemed much longer. At his implied invitation, I stepped past him and entered the room, where I sank into a chair and looked inquiringly up at him.

Springer came a few steps into the room. Kennedy stood on the threshold, one hand on the open door.

Springer said, "There's no point in disturbing you tonight. We'll pick you up early in the morning and go down to headquarters." He started to turn around.

I said, "Just a minute, Mr. Springer. I am confused by this—this courtesy. Are you really concerned over whether or not I get a good night's sleep?"

Springer surprised me by looking rather flustered. He said, "Well, of course—That is, we—"

Kennedy, the Silent, said succinctly, "Our superior is flying here from out of the city. He has been away on—business. There is no point in proceeding without him, and he will not arrive in town until early tomorrow morning."

"Ah. That makes better sense. But why didn't you leave me with the police?"

"Their belief is that you had nothing to do with Miss Stetson's death. Your fingerprints were on an engagement book, on a few photographs, and on the door-knob to the apartment, outside and inside. There were none in the bathroom. Unless you premeditatedly wore gloves for part of the time and then discarded and disposed of them at the proper moment, you did not commit the murder. The police were not prepared to believe you did. Besides, we vouched for your safekeeping and expressed our interest in the case.

We feel certain that you were not in New York at the time of the Stetson murder. You can tell us about it tomorrow."

"But why didn't you let them hold me as a witness?"

"Contrary to popular notions, the police don't like to involve themselves in anything that might resemble false arrest. And besides—" Mr. Kennedy paused. Then he said firmly, "We—Springer and I—preferred not to have you offer them any explanations. If you were faced with a cell you might have changed your mind and given them a truthful explanation of your—involvement."

"I see." And, to a minute degree, I did. "And what's to prevent me from leaving here now?"

Mr. Kennedy smiled pleasantly. "We telephoned the hotel before we were, uh, introduced to you, and arranged to occupy the room next door for the night. We'd really prefer that you do not leave."

He stood aside for Springer to pass him, and then he put his hand on the key Springer had left in the lock. For an angry second I thought he was going to lock me in the room. I should have known better; Kennedy, and Springer, were much too smooth for so crude a gesture. Instead, he transferred the key to the inside of the lock, said "Good night," and closed the door.

20

FOR five minutes after it had closed behind Springer and Kennedy I sat motionless, staring blankly at the uncommunicative surface of the door. Then I got up and turned the key in the lock.

My momentary impulse towards flight had passed quickly. Setting aside the fact that I doubted if it would be possible—the two men's competence was very apparent and I felt certain that measures to prevent my escape had been carefully taken—I could see no next step, no avenue left for me to explore. My mind could carry me through the first motions—into the hotel corridor, down the lift, through the lobby—but when I pictured myself in the street, my mind baulked at further imagining.

I had never been fleeing *from*; I had been working *towards*. Towards Ellen, I had desperately hoped. And what had I found? A wounded Natasha Giroux, a murdered Stephanie Stetson.

But not Ellen.

It had been a long and unusual day. I was asleep within ten minutes after Kennedy and Springer left me.

But the next day started for me at six-thirty in the morning. That was not too surprising; I had had eight hours' sleep. I felt alert, removed from the more flabbergasting aspects of the previous day's experience, hungry, and energetic.

I sent for and ate breakfast, and then, without dressing, I sat beside the window and looked out over the city at a magnificent expanse of river blanketed by a morning fog that was waging a losing battle with a brilliant sun. It was comparatively cool beside the window, and the traffic noises which, at nine o'clock on the previous morning, had overcome the great gap between my room and the distant street, were far less intrusive now, at seven-thirty.

I felt calm and hopeful. The night before I had come to the conclusion, which still seemed sensible, inevitable, to me, that there were no further steps for me to take, no avenues to explore. Well, then, the time had come to think, to unravel the web of half-fact, half-confusion I had picked up.

What was basic, pertinent?

Well, start with Ellen. That was the beginning.

What did I know about Ellen? So little, so very little. She was a teacher. She was a teacher of history and geography. She lived in New York City. She had the power of total recall. I loved her very much. And that's all I really knew.

History. She taught history. She had sent a message: go to four towns—Albany, Syracuse, Utica, Binghamton. I'd had a classical education and she'd been a history teacher. If it hadn't been for Binghamton I'd have worked on the classical implications. But Binghamton was the least classical reference I could think of, and my imagination baulked at trying to fit it into that pattern.

What about geography? I recalled one of the statements she had made over dinner in the Adlon. When she was attempting to explain her phenomenal memory, she had said: "I can reproduce a map, although I have very little drawing ability."

I got my maps out of the bureau drawer and looked at New York State, at my four crosses. Did the distances mean anything? From New York City—I added another cross—to Albany; a hundred and fifty miles. From Albany to Syracuse; another hundred and fifty miles. But that promising mathematical coincidence broke down on the next junket. From Syracuse to Utica was only fifty miles or so.

And then I stared at the map. I hadn't known anything about New York State. The strangeness of that itinerary had not occurred to me until that minute. I had first gone due north. Then northwest. But in travelling to Syracuse, Natasha and I had passed right through Utica. Then we had returned to it. Why? Binghamton was south, closer, if anything, to Syracuse, so that couldn't be the reason. Why?

I took my pencil and drew a line from New York to Albany. Then I finished outlining the itinerary. From Albany to Syracuse, back to Utica, and then down to Binghamton.

There, traced on my map, was a neat outline. It said, "77."

I was getting excited. I didn't quite know what I had, but—and then a knock on my door interrupted me. I opened the door, assuming the waiter had come for the tray.

Springer and Kennedy, looking immaculate, stood there in what eventually came to be an identifying pose for me. To this day, the FBI is personified for me by the image of two pleasant but expressionless young men, looking immaculate, their hats in their hands, standing politely on an anonymous threshold.

Involuntarily I glanced down at my watch. It was a few minutes before eight o'clock.

Springer said, "Did we awaken you? No, I see you've had your breakfast. May we—?"

I said, "Certainly. Come in. I was a bit surprised because—well, isn't it rather early?"

"Yes, I guess it is, but if you don't mind we'd like to get going."

"Very well, then. If you'll sit down for a few minutes, I'll dress."

They had a knack of looking quite comfortable where-ever they happened to perch. As they sat in that hotel room at eight o'clock on an increasingly hot morning, they might, if it weren't for their neat business attire, have been two friends who, coming to fetch me for a golf date, had found me oversleeping.

There was silence in the room for two or three minutes. Their imperturbability intrigued and slightly irritated me; I wondered if it was unfailingly with them.

As I pulled on my trousers I asked a question born of that curiosity: "Were you in Utica yesterday when the inquiry from the New York police came through?"

Springer examined the question and apparently found it harmless. He said, "No. We are attached to the New York office of the Bureau. Anyway, the New York City police did not forward an inquiry through to the police in Utica."

I looked up from the shirt I was trying to detach from its cardboard stiffener. I was entirely confused and I suppose I showed it. At any rate, although I said nothing Springer answered the inquiry on my face.

"They would, of course, have checked with Utica very soon, acting on your statement, but first they sent a routine request on your fingerprints to Washington, and Washington instantly alerted us—that is, the New York bureau."

"Washington? The capital? *My* fingerprints?"

"Why, yes, Mr. Terrant. We—that is, the CIA—have an, uh, extensive file on the Content case and all its ramifications. Your report to the Divisional Superintendent of the Special Branch of Scotland Yard is naturally a part of that file. In their usual thorough way, Scotland Yard included your prints with the report they sent us—and, of course, the FBI had been scouring the entire East for you since night before last, anyway. So we were very much alerted."

"You had been looking for me? By name, you mean? You were looking for a John Terrant?"

"Why, yes." It was his turn to look surprised. "Certainly Mr. Terrant. We should never have lost you after you left the hotel, of course. The trouble was that when you boarded the truck that night the operators following you didn't have any means of conveyance. They had had to park their car a long time before, because, as I understand it, you wandered around on foot for a number of hours, and they would have been conspicuous if they had been driving.

"When they had subdued the pair who showed up behind you—subdued them without, I'm told, any help from you—"

I couldn't keep silent. "Do you mean that some of the participants in that ludicrous street battle represented the United States Government?"

"Well, that's one way of putting it. Yes."

"But why didn't they say so?"

There was a little pause, and then Mr. Springer asked succinctly, "When?"

"Ah—" I trailed off.

"That's the point, you see. The two men following you made a good move when they enlisted you on their side. As I understand it, you delivered the first blow, and quite a blow, at that."

"Ah, yes, I suppose so."

Mr. Springer's face was impassive, and he didn't sound annoyed, but he wasn't willing to leave it at that. "Besides which," he added, "even when Kennedy and I removed you from police head-quarters—obviously with the permission of the police—and then when we showed you our credentials you weren't easy to persuade on the subject of our identity; I really feel that at 1 a.m. on a deserted dirt road, it would have been considerably more difficult to convince you?"

He waited politely, but I had nothing to say.

He resumed: "After you had stopped—helping—however, our men overcame the pair. They are now in the Utica jail, where we shall hold them for the time being.

"By then it was too late to catch up with you. All our men knew was that you had got a ride on an eastbound truck. Our search, thereafter, concentrated on—"

I interrupted, "But why, in the first place, did your men follow me like that? Why didn't they simply catch up with me before the confusion of the street fight made it impossible and explain calmly exactly who they were?"

"Well, Mr. Terrant, the hotel lobby was a rather unexpected place for John Terrant to turn up in. It seemed sensible to let your actions speak for themselves. Then, at the counter in the luncheon-ette, when you exposed your intention of going to the hospital, our man realized that you could be of real help. Mrs. Giroux had refused to give any information or explanation to the police or to us. She would have talked eventually, of course. But whenever we can speed things up it's sensible to do so. And it seemed likely that she *would* talk to you. So our man left the luncheonette ahead of you and called the hospital, and we stationed two police stenographers behind the air vent of Mrs. Giroux's room. We also—uh—smoothed your way. The transcript of your conversation with Natasha Giroux will be of inestimable assistance."

I felt bitter. I had a vivid picture of the receptionist's swinging chair and the man walking away from me down the hospital corridor. Probably J. Edgar Hoover.

I had gone into the bathroom to comb my hair, and I called back, "Ah, yes." I was beginning to feel rather foolish.

I added, "But I don't really understand how they identified me in the hotel lobby. That I was in some way implicated was fairly obvious, I suppose, but how in the world did they know who I was?"

There was silence in the other room. Mr. Springer cleared his throat. Then Mr. Kennedy's quiet voice took over. "We do have the file on you as a part of the Content case, Mr. Terrant. It is true we didn't know you were in America, but when our man saw you in the hotel lobby—You know, Mr. Terrant, you make a very distinctive appearance—your height, your physique, your unusually clear, fair colouring. And when you add to that your accent—"

There was quiet again for a minute, and then Mr. Kennedy added, and I couldn't detect the slightest trace of amusement in his carefully flat tones—"in spite of your toothache."

I looked in the bathroom mirror and felt like a damned fool.

21

THE FBI office was far more anonymous than my hotel room. There wasn't a luxury in it. It was furnished with grey-steel filing cabinets and a tan-steel desk, and blocks of dark-grey marbleized linoleum covered the floor.

Kennedy, Springer, and I sat in tan and grey leather chairs facing the man behind the desk. His name was Roma, and he was perhaps forty-five years old. He was movie-star handsome, but that didn't prevent him from having the same air of quiet competence as his two assistants. The air, in fact, was carried in him to a much farther degree. It struck me, as I looked at him, that he was the essence of impersonality.

He had said, "How do you do, Mr. Terrant. Won't you sit down?" I murmured a polite reply, and then we sat and looked at each other.

He finally broke the silence. "You have been—uh—very difficult to—to—" He stopped there. I imagine that he was running through the available verbs and discarding each of them in turn—catch, trap, snare, apprehend—?

He gave it up and went on to a further thought. "There is a Divisional Superintendent of Scotland Yard who seems to feel somewhat as we do. Some British governmental agency—I don't know which one—in a routine check of newspapers, picked up a mention of an 'Ellen Content' who was supposed to be sailing for America. But by the time their report filtered through to the British Secret Service, to the correct division of Scotland Yard, to the CIA, and then to us the ship had docked here some time before. However, the information does seem to have started a Superintendent Jelliffson on a search for you."

I said, "Indeed?"

Roma eyed me as if that comment struck him as being insufficient. He said, and a barely perceptible note of persuasiveness had been added to his impersonal voice, "Mr. Terrant, I'm going to put our cards on the table. Then I hope you will do the same."

There was a lingering question mark in the air. I said, "I can't promise anything until I know what you ask—"

"Of course. Well, let us start with the murder of Stephanie Stetson. We—you—must supply the New York police with satisfactory evidence that you are not involved, and, certainly, that you are not in any way responsible. If, of course, you are not."

His impersonality had a very chilling quality. I asked, "When exactly was she killed?"

"That is not easy to be exact about. But we know it was in an uncomfortably close time relationship to your arrival. We know that Mrs. Giroux arrived here on Tuesday morning and left immediately for Albany. Her story from there on is explicit as to time and place. Her movements are being checked, but it is already certain that she is in the clear. You, it would seem, arrived here very soon after her. Miss Stetson was killed the night of your arrival, or in the early hours of the next morning—after midnight Tuesday and before dawn on Wednesday. It is impossible, because of the heat and the amount of time that has elapsed, for the medical authorities to be more specific than that."

"I see." I thought it over. "At eleven o'clock that night I talked with a cab driver of the Sunbeam Taxi Company—*he* called *me* at my hotel." I thought of the £17 and added, "He will undoubtedly remember the incident.

"Thereafter, until I boarded a train for Albany at two thirty-five in the morning, I spent my time being telephoned by, telephoning to, or standing at, the hotel desk trying to arrange a seat to Albany. I don't think the calls were ever more than fifteen minutes apart."

"I see. That sounds sufficient. We'll check it and give the data to the police.

"Now, yesterday you went to Miss Stetson's apartment. Incidentally, in the natural course of events we would have arrived at that apartment very shortly. We, too, had noted the reference to Miss Stetson and the St. Regis in the account of her experiences that Natasha Giroux gave you. However, we were concentrating most of our energy on finding you. That seemed like the most important first step.

"But how did you find the Stetson apartment? The St. Regis Hotel, which was all the address you had, tell us they knew nothing about a Stephanie Stetson, did not know where to find her, and so could not and did not give you any help."

"I looked it up in the telephone book."

Mr. Roma looked even more like a moving-picture hero when he smiled, although the smile was brief and a little twisted. He said, "Admirably direct. Presumably your—predecessors—did the same thing." His face reverted to gravity, and he spoke a little more slowly. "But this direct route bolsters my growing conviction that that poor woman was completely without involvement in the disappearance of Miss Content."

"How could she be? Natasha's message—"

"She could be the *wrong* Stephanie Stetson. The details of this Miss Stetson's life are unrolling before the investigations of the police and the FBI in an unusually forthright way. Most people have strange twists and turns to their lives, but not Miss Stetson. There is growing evidence that she was simply and exactly what she appeared to be: a solitary, middle-aged spinster, once possessed of a quite good soprano voice, now reduced to teaching music. There are no involvements, no convolutions to the pattern. So far there isn't a breath, a suspicion, a thought of a political connexion. I doubt if the Stephanie Stetson who is rapidly being drawn for us ever had a political thought in her life—let alone a conviction. I suppose it's too soon to be sure, but we'll see; we'll find out.

"Now, as to the background of this whole affair, and your part in it." He paused, and the slight note of sympathy that had softened his voice as he discussed Miss Stetson disappeared. "We know something about you. We know of your acquaintance with Miss

Content. Our reports don't make it clear how long you had known each other, but it is our impression that the friendship was of short duration?"

The question mark was hung out again. I simply sat still and looked interested.

Mr. Roma's imperturbable face didn't change, but he seemed to sigh slightly before he went on: "Because that friendship existed at all, we have gathered certain data on you. We know your age, your profession, the details of your background, the part of England you were brought up in; two years ago we checked on your friends, your employment record, your political affiliations, your—"

I interrupted: "Let's boil it down to 'dossier.' I accept the fact that you know all about me, and I must add that it must be the dullest record in your files. But you started this conversation by saying you were going to put your cards on the table. Telling me about me is not really supplying me with any playing cards."

Mr. Roma shook his head. "You really have an amazing ability to underestimate yourself, Mr. Terrant. Our records are very complete, and yours is an extremely interesting one. Your war record, Mr. Terrant. Very admirable. Your ability in your work—didn't you win the Alcost International prize in the field of reporting? Even your scholastic standing—"

Mr. Roma cleared his throat. "I reviewed these matters because I am of two minds as to the advisability of the step I'm about to take—that is, laying my cards on the table. Your war record, your work record, your scholastic record—everything up to 1948—would lead one to believe that you are extremely trustworthy. From 1948 on, you have been—appallingly foolhardy. Therefore it seems wisest to explain the situation to you and then appeal to your intelligence to overcome your foolhardiness.

"After I have explained the situation and have elicited whatever information you can give me, I want you to go back to your hotel, Mr. Terrant, and I want you to stay there."

The suggestion had a familiar ring. I felt as if I were back in the morass of Berlin. The endless hopelessness and unproductiveness of the Berlin experience was something I could not, *would* not, suffer through again. I would *not* be a patient, obedient bystander.

My face must have mirrored my rebellion, because Mr. Roma's voice became almost imperceptibly sterner. "You already have been involved in one street fight and one murder," he added. "If you don't follow my advice you are either going to get seriously in our way and hamper us in accomplishing our mutual ends, or you are going to get yourself killed. As a matter of fact, it is rather amazing that you are alive now."

No amount of conversation was going to sway me from my resolve to see the thing through. I said, "But I *am* alive now, and I am patiently awaiting the cards."

It was obvious that Mr. Roma knew what I was thinking and planning, and it was just as obvious that he didn't like it. But after a moment during which he eyed me impassively, he merely said, "All right, Mr. Terrant. Well, then, we have the record of your conversation with Mr. Russell, to whom you spoke early in 1948 in Berlin. So we know what Mr. Russell told you, and we know what Mr. Benjamin later told you. We also have your own outline of the facts as you gave it to Scotland Yard. Presumably all you haven't been told—since Miss Content was a most trustworthy person—is what touched the fuse to the whole affair?"

This time I was glad to put an end to the question mark. "I don't know what happened in Berlin. I don't know what the Natasha business is all about. But, with all due respect to your trust in Miss Content, you would know of my ignorance from the recording of my talk with Natasha Giroux." Perhaps it was childish of me.

Roma said stiffly, "Quite so. Well, 'the Natasha business' is something of a misnomer because Natasha Giroux is an innocent bystander. As much so as you. More so than Miss Content. Mrs. Giroux's father ran a restaurant. It was a Russian type of place, Russian food, Russian entertainment—logically enough since he was born and grew up in Russia. By coincidence it fell in the Russian zone when the partitioning of Berlin took place. Then logic again stepped in when it began to be patronized, after the partition, by Russians. But eventually logic took a blow and human nature came to the fore. Some Russian, some very highly placed Russian—one who probably travelled incognito and who we probably never knew was in

Berlin—while visiting that café one night, talked too much. Even that wasn't important because he had a private room. But he got carried away by his eloquence and made his points *on the tablecloth*. Mr. Paviloff found that tablecloth and understood its significance. He painstakingly memorized what it said, personally supervised its burning, and then went to the American authorities. Miss Content was assigned to the case because of her knowledge of Russian.

"The importance of the information which that tablecloth contained is so great, Mr. Terrant"—Mr. Roma leaned forward a quarter of an inch—"that my orders are to do anything, anything within our power, to recapture it. Its secrecy is so great that I have absolutely no idea what it's about. I understand that there are only three men in the United States who do know what it concerns.

"Ours is not a silly organization. We are never, for instance, kept in ignorance of what we are striving towards. The fact that we have not been told of the subject matter of this—information—brings home to me, with great weight, how vastly important it must be."

A thought that had been teasing me came out: "What about William Eider? Didn't he know—hadn't he and Miss Content discussed the whole business?"

"We think he knew all about it. But he didn't have Miss Content's memory, and they seem to have been afraid to commit any of it to paper. Some of—"

"'*Didn't*' have her memory? Did something happen to William Eider?"

Mr. Roma stared at me. Then he said slowly, "I assumed that Mr. Russell or Mr. Benjamin—I suppose they were quite correct to conceal it." He looked reflective.

"Conceal *what*?"

"William Eider was run over by a truck less than twenty-four hours after he talked with you, Mr. Terrant. He did not know Miss Content was not safe, but there were indications that he had anticipated his own—misadventure. As I understand it, his coded notes looked as if he had been struggling to reconstruct something. The CIA listed his death under a false name to avoid awkward questions from the Press."

I had a sudden, vivid recollection of William Eider's exhausted face and a shamed realization of how he must have been trying to beat his assassins out at the very time that he was being patient with me. He *had* known the danger; he had warned me of it.

Mr. Roma said, "Well, getting back to Mr. Paviloff—some of the rest we shall never know. Why, for instance, the Russians suddenly awakened to their error. Probably someone else in the restaurant reported the mysterious burning. However, by the time Paviloff reached Miss Content, almost twenty-four hours had passed, and she was quite right in estimating that he was probably secure and undetected. She correctly evaluated the importance of what he had told her, and she arranged to get him out of the country to the proper authorities. His wife and daughter, to whom he never told a word of what he knew or what it was about, were to leave also—in the name of simple humanity.

"But the Russians found out. They went to the house and killed Paviloff. They didn't dare take the chance of believing his protestations as to his family's ignorance. And that was their big mistake, because while they were out looking for Natasha Paviloff, Miss Content memorized his information."

I said, "The litany!"

Mr. Roma said, "I beg your pardon?"

I shook my head. "Nothing really. I just remembered—Do go on."

"That's all."

The familiar feeling of outrage—of being promised something that was not delivered—was coming over me, I took a tight rein and said, "I'm afraid I don't agree with you. You've left something out: where is Ellen Content?"

"Both Mr. Russell and Mr. Benjamin explained our position on that to you. We don't think she ever arrived here."

I do not know exactly what happened to me at that moment. I did not anticipate it then, and I find it hard to account for now. But quite unexpectedly I was standing, and I was definitely shouting. And until I realized what I was doing, I punctuated each sentence by slamming my fist on the tan steel desk.

"I'm tired of it! Very tired of it! *You* don't think she arrived here. Russell—Benjamin—Jelliffson—you all 'don't think.' You all think she's dead. Well, what in the name of God do *I* care what *you* think? Do you also think I'm a fool? Why do you think I'm running around, struggling around, looking around for her? If she's dead? I'll tell you why—it's because I *know* she isn't dead. I *know*. . . . Think, think, think! You all think too much and feel too little—"

The steel desk hurt my hand. And somewhere within my vision Springer's and Kennedy's faces joined Roma's. Roma's face had changed very little, but Kennedy and Springer looked utterly astounded. That hurt, too. I had made a spectacle of myself. I had behaved—

I sat down. I put my hand in my lap. I said in an even tone, "What about the message to Natasha?"

The silence lasted only a fraction of a second. Then Mr. Roma sat back in his chair, and it seemed to me that he withdrew even further than that. He said, "Yes. Well, the minute a routine inquiry came through the day before yesterday from Utica on an 'Ellen Content,' we rushed men to Utica. They spotted you in the lobby of the hotel. Since then we have checked through the Bank of England, and we understand how you happen to be here. We have the story Mrs. Giroux told you, and if there is anything in it, we'll find out—"

I was well in control of myself by then, but I couldn't let that pass unchallenged. "But of course there's something in it!" I said. "What of the murder of Stephanie Stetson? It seems to me that is a fact, a stark *fact*. And what possible sense would there be in sending Natasha on a wild-goose chase unless there was a reason, and what reason could there be other than something to do with Ellen?"

"We are endeavouring to find the answers to those questions. Meanwhile I've had you brought here for two reasons. First, to request you to stop—well, meddling is a rude word, but I'm afraid it applies. And second, to find out if there is anything you know that could help us. You have followed Mrs. Giroux; we haven't. You have been over the territory; we haven't. You saw Mr. Paviloff the night he died; we didn't. You got to the scene of Stephanie

Stetson's murder before we did. Frankly speaking, I don't believe you are in possession of a single fact that is unknown to us, but if you do know anything, I urge your cooperation."

In the longish pause that followed, I added to my shaken condition an awareness of the fact that, although I was firmly set against telling Mr. Roma anything, he was right in his surmise that I didn't know a single thing to tell. So much for the stories and the novels, I thought, in which the protagonist always withholds information from the authorities, information usually referred to as "an ace up his sleeve." In this game of laying of cards, I was handicapped: no ace.

I said abruptly, "Didn't the CIA give their people instructions on all contingencies?"

Mr. Roma looked remotely interested. "Why, yes, I suppose so. What specifically are you thinking of?"

"Well, suppose someone was held, kidnapped, hidden away? What message would he try to get out?"

"Mr. Terrant, the CIA and the FBI operate on a basis of complete common sense. Such a contingency doesn't require a code. Presumably that person would not be able to employ fancy methods. He'd simply try to get his location, his address, through."

Suddenly I felt excitement growing in me. "Doesn't it occur to you that the trip Natasha and I just took through New York State might have been that address?"

Mr. Roma's interest had died. "Of course it occurs to us."

"It might constitute some kind of message."

"It might."

"Well, *do* something to figure it out, then!"

"Downstairs"—Mr. Roma spoke quietly—"the best decoders in America are working on the possibilities implied by that trip. They have been at it ever since Mrs. Giroux, faced with the transcript of her conversation with you, gave us the complete story of her tour. We're doing something, Mr. Terrant."

"Well, what about the murder of Miss Stetson? What is the connexion there? What—"

"The FBI is cooperating with the New York police in an attempt to solve that murder. We are hampered by the elapsed time and the irrelevance of the murder, its *non sequitur* quality. As I told you,

I have a strong suspicion that the wrong woman was killed. So still another of the moves we are making is a search for another woman by that name." Then, surprisingly, he looked vaguely alarmed. "But, Mr. Terrant, if you have any notion of instituting a private search of your own, discard it. We are equipped; you are not. If I suspect you of harbouring any such notion I shall have you restrained."

It was the first outward threat. I responded to it in the fashion of British nationals the world over. "I am an Englishman, Mr. Roma. I am not subject—"

His voice didn't rise, but his interruption had that effect. "You are most certainly subject to the laws of this country. Considering that you are a newspaperman, you must be aware of that. You have been involved in a murder. In view of that fact, your government would not think of interfering, unless we abused you outside the provinces of our own law. But I would not have to resort to the subterfuge of holding you in connexion with the murder—and it would be a subterfuge, since I do not think you are in any way involved in Miss Stetson's death—but as I say, I would not have to resort to subterfuges because I already have the entire sympathy of your government in the matter of handling you. I am told that they advised you—that they bluntly *ordered* you—to stay out of the matter. You ignored them. The Superintendent Jelliffson I mentioned is extremely irate. He will be most sympathetic to any steps I see fit to take, and I gather that he is very influential." Roma's steely impersonality was uncomfortably convincing.

"Now, will you please answer my question: is there anything you know, anything you've picked up in your—extensive travels, that might possibly be of help to us?"

I sat still for a bit, and then I said, "Yes. Ellen Content is on Seventy-seventh Street."

22

Mr. Roma's handsome impassivity quivered. There was a rustle as Kennedy and Springer, who had been absolutely silent and almost motionless since we entered the room, transferred their gaze from the brilliant blue haze over Manhattan to me.

Mr. Roma said, "I beg your pardon?"

"Listen," I said. "It wasn't the *wrong* Stephanie Stetson; there wasn't *any* Stephanie Stetson. It *must* have been that way. Listen—" I stopped the too-fast flow of words and tried to assemble my thoughts. Then I said, "'Ask for two letters in the name of Stephanie Stetson.' Doesn't that sound odd to you? People don't go to hotel desks and ask for *two* letters—they ask if there are *any* letters. But if you stop to think of 'two letters' in the name that has repeatedly struck me as being almost ridiculously alliterative— Stephanie Stetson of the St. Regis—you are instantly faced with *s-t, s-t, s-t*. And *s-t*, in addition to being the abbreviation for 'saint,' is the abbreviation for 'street.' As you said, the only sensible message is an address. Ellen could not have foreseen that someone would bear that name; she simply invented it so she could get across to us the idea of 'street.' And then she spelled out seventy-seven for us—Could someone get me a map of New York State?"

Mr. Kennedy instantly left the room.

I went on: "Natasha started in New York City; she was to end her trip in New York City. Ellen was a New Yorker. Where else could the street be but in New York City? I'll wager that those small towns don't *have* a Seventy-seventh Street."

118

Mr. Kennedy returned with a map and a young man.

"Here." I grabbed the map. "Here." I took a blotter off Mr. Roma's desk and laid it on the map, using its straight edge as a ruler. The young man who had just entered the room put a pencil into my waving hand. I drew a line from New York to Albany and from Albany to Syracuse. "Then from Syracuse to Utica to Binghamton. Seventy-seven." I put the pencil down and sat back in my chair.

Mr. Roma, Mr. Kennedy, Mr. Springer, and the young man stood grouped around me, circling me, all half-stooped as they looked at the map. No one said a word. Mr. Roma looked up at the strange young man, who looked back at him. Then Mr. Roma let himself down in his chair, Kennedy and Springer resumed their seats, and the young man perched on the window-sill. But the tension in the room didn't lessen.

Mr. Roma said, "Yes." He seemed a little less remote. "Yes, it's possible. We'll work on it. Now, may we have your word that you'll return to your hotel and stay there?"

The sound that came out of me surprised me. It was almost a sob, but it formed the words, "No, no, no!"

Mr. Roma said, "Thank you, Arthur," to the young man on the window-sill. And to Kennedy and Springer, "I don't think we need hold you boys up any longer."

In a minute he and I were alone in the room.

Roma leaned across his desk towards me. The impassivity of his features was undisturbed, but his eyes—large, black eyes—seemed more alive. He said, "Look, Mr. Terrant. I am not insensible to your concern. Your feeling for Miss Content is—uh—recorded in the files. I—sympathize, believe me. But there is really nothing you can do. We'll do everything in the world we can. Forgetting the importance of the matter as it applies to the interests of the United States, we, too, feel a—human feeling towards Miss Content. She was one of us. She was engaged in helping her country. We will do everything we can, believe me.

"But as far as you are concerned. . . Don't you see that you've been miraculously lucky? It's understandable, if you trace back over your movements. I think the Russians simply don't know you exist.

They had no way of knowing you were in the Paviloff house that night. And so they didn't know you delivered Mrs. Paviloff to us. As you travelled around after Mrs. Giroux you were far enough behind so that your investigations came after they had left. And we have—incommunicado—those two men who did catch up with you the other night. They aren't going to be reporting to anyone about anything for a long time to come. So you are in the clear. The Russians just don't know about you. But if you continue on this stubborn pursuit they will learn about you. It is absolutely inevitable. And then your chances of continuing to live will be no better than—than Edward Bigeby's and William Eider's.

"Look at what they did to the Stetson woman. There could have been no reason for that murder, except the outside possibility that she would be able to identify them. They had found their way there, so they must have reasoned that someone else might also. That was sound enough, but what difference could it have made if we did find her? Suppose she told you or us that two men came to see her—or four men? That they asked incomprehensible questions? Her very lack of involvement, lack of understanding, would have been a block to a cogent report. Suppose she told us they were tall, or short, or overweight or underweight? Or that one had a mole on his chin, or that his eyes were dark brown? Would such infor-mation have done us a particle of good?

"Even if we had caught someone and she had identified them, it wouldn't have constituted a real jeopardy to them. Because she wouldn't, couldn't finger them for any crime, or produce a tape recording of their questions, even if they were illuminating.

"They killed her because to them life is cheap, the individual has no value, the purge is commonplace, and in ruthlessness lies pride.

"They have caught up with you once, Mr. Terrant. In Utica. Now you're ahead of the game. If you continue to place yourself in their path your life isn't worth a matchstick. Give us a chance, Mr. Terrant."

I didn't feel bitter any longer—or in pain, or in revolt. I was simply numb and exhausted, like a child after a storm of tears. My voice, when it came, sounded flat and expressionless. I said, "With all due politeness—" It didn't sound right. "I don't mean that as sarcasm. Please accept my words at face value.

"So—at face value—you leave me two things to say. As unemotionally as possible I should like to point out that my life *isn't* worth a matchstick without Ellen Content. I know; I've had two years in which to learn that lesson. So, in a very real sense, I have nothing to lose. And second, giving you 'a chance' seems to be doing just that—taking a chance. Because, you see, you have not made progress so far. You did not pick up Natasha when she arrived here, you did not find Stephanie Stetson, you did not decipher the seventy-seven. . . ."

Roma was not annoyed. He said, "All true, all very true. I can certainly understand how you might feel, what implications you might draw from those facts. But if you'll think it through, you'll realize that until now you have had an appreciable head start— whereas now we are even with you. And—starting even—we have a tremendous advantage. We are trained to this kind of work, we have informants, technical knowledge, entrée, forces of men. I really think—" He broke off and looked at me with a trace of concern.

"You are not well," he said. "Please, Mr. Terrant. Give us that chance. I promise we'll advise you as soon as there is something to say. Go to the hotel."

There was nothing more to be said. There was common sense and truth in his defence. Besides, it was nice of him. He didn't have to request or explain. He could have held me—

I stood up and started towards the door. I felt entirely numb.

As I neared the door, Mr. Roma came up beside me and put his hand on the door-knob before I could reach for it. He put his other hand on my arm in a gesture of pure compassion. I was startled by the warmth of his eyes. And then he smiled, a completely human, sweet smile that lighted and lifted his whole face, bringing it into focus with his eyes.

He said, "I'll hope, too, Mr. Terrant."

23

THE hotel room was a cage. A hot cage. I pushed at the food on my luncheon tray. I took a cold shower. I ceaselessly adjusted and readjusted the venetian blinds, trying to catch the air and bar the sun. The bed was too hot to lie on, the chair was too prickly to sit in. And always before me was Ellen's small face, young and soft in its outlines, with its clear, brave, intelligent eyes. I had a great desire to sleep as a form of escape, but my night had been a good and restful one. I was inexorably awake.

I finally went to the bureau, got out my maps, spread them open on the bed, and drew up a chair. The map of New York State stared blankly back at me. On it was the big "77" I had traced there, and it yielded nothing else.

But the map of New York City was comparatively new territory to me. Manhattan Island, an amoeba-shaped swatch of land, had amoeba-like cilia sticking out from its every side—bridges, tunnels, ferries. The plan of the city itself was, to a Londoner, surprisingly neat. It had squares it's true, not unlike London's—but they merely punctuated and didn't confuse the neat pattern of its rectangular blocks. A few of its avenues, stretching from north to south, crossed and recrossed each other, but its side streets, mostly numbered, ran true—from east to west, from one river to the other. And there, almost bisecting the amoeba, was the line marked "Seventy-seventh Street."

I started to dress.

In the course of that afternoon I learned a good deal about that particular black line. You could walk Seventy-seventh Street's few miles, from river to river, in not much over an hour. Its east portion—from the East River Drive to Fifth Avenue—was largely elegance. First came beautiful town houses with polished brass, old shady trees, quiet and peace. Around Park Avenue I encountered vast but still quiet apartment houses, equipped with canopies and doormen. Near Fifth Avenue the town houses came again—more formidable now, magnificent stone structures that spoke of old wealth.

At Fifth Avenue, the rectangle that is Central Park interrupted my tour. Here I went south to a Park entrance, walked through the pretty, rather formal park, and, emerging on the other side, went a few blocks up the wide avenue called Central Park West to Seventy-seventh again.

From there on Seventy-seventh Street's elegance disintegrated. Old brownstones, so aptly named, stretched in long, monotonous rows. On the east side of the park, the brownstones' long flights of brown steps had been torn away and new faces, set with beautifully proportioned doors, had been superimposed. But here on the West Side the stoops and their long stair-appendages remained. The effect was dreary. House after house carried signs, "Rooms to Rent." From Central Park West to the Hudson River dead end—four immense squares—were the rooming houses, dingy hotels, and great apartment buildings, fifty or so years old, built in a period of rococo splendour that had now gone to sooty seed.

I went to bed at midnight, as tired as I had ever been, without a constructive idea in my head.

But after breakfast in the morning, I felt clearheaded and determined. I remembered Natasha's action in the hotel lobby in Utica. "Foolish," she had called it. Well, perhaps it was. Dangerous, too. But its directness had got action. She had flushed her quarry. Perhaps if *I* could get *myself* shot we would be, Mr. Roma to the contrary, another step forward instead of swimming in a black sea of nothing, nothing.

I started at the west side this time. Its dinginess seemed more promising for the project I had in mind.

The cab driver set me down on the corner of Riverside Drive and Seventy-seventh and drove off. After a minute I started up the north side of the street on foot.

My plan was about as simple as a plan could be. I rang door-bells, knocked on doors, poked my head into offices, and asked a single question: "Is there a Miss Ellen Content here?"

By noon, I had learned a good deal, I thought. If Ellen *were* in any of those places I would know by the way in which I was answered. Because people did not say "No"—flatly, as I imagined Ellen's possible jailers would. Instead they first looked blank; they said, "What number did you want?" then they said, "What was that name?" and *then,* abruptly or apologetically, according to their natures, they said, "No." This formula was almost unvaried.

At noon I retreated to a cross street and had a dreadful cup of coffee and an even more dreadful sandwich in a place that called itself a "luncheonette."

Then I strolled the few steps back to Seventy-seventh and contemplated the possibilities.

By skipping over the apartment houses and hotels I had almost reached Central Park. It had seemed unlikely to me that large hostelries would be a sensible place in which to set up a hidden jail. But now I wondered: should I go back and make a clean sweep? And if I tried it, would desk clerks and lift men permit such an invasion?

And then suddenly, without reason, I knew. Perhaps it was the repetition of the "luncheonette" that looked so much like the place in Utica in which I had had coffee. In Utica a man had paid for his coffee before I did, and then he had left the place. I had had no suspicion whatever that he was following me. And I don't remember his having entered. But, from Springer's comments, it was clear that he had been an FBI man.

Now, what had just happened in that luncheonette? I couldn't untangle it. The long counter had been crowded, and by an odd batch of men—some white-collared, some rough-shirted, all reduced to similarity by the common denominator of the heat.

But I was being followed. Whether I was an amateur or not, that I knew.

I stood indecisively on the street corner and ran mentally through all the ruses I had ever heard of or read about. If I could manoeuvre myself to a store window I could look behind me—or so I had always understood. But that, I realized, was more easily written about than accomplished. Store windows give one an excellent view of the opposite side of the street. Besides, how could I differentiate between the people—some aimless, some purposeful—going up and down the busy avenue?

I stood still on the corner and thought it over. I came up with a surprising conclusion: what did I care who was following me? What did I need ruses for? Being followed was perfect, it was wonderful; I had flushed the quarry.

But having flushed it, what? It was very brave and derring-do of me to decide that I'd get shot. I'd get shot; I'd die. Or I'd get shot and I'd live and be taken off to a hospital—and what possible good would I have accomplished?

I crossed the avenue, entered a pharmacy (or so it said on the window; it looked like an odds-and-ends shop to me), and practised my newly acquired knowledge on the Manhattan telephone book. I was put through to Mr. Roma rather quickly.

"This is Terrant, Mr. Roma. I am being followed." It was my day for being direct.

There was the characteristic pause and then the characteristic dryness of voice. Roma said, "Around your hotel room?"

"Ah, no. I've been out—"

Roma said, "Just a minute, please, Mr. Terrant. I'm wanted on another wire."

There was a small wait, and then he came back on the wire. "So you are out and you are being followed, Mr. Terrant? That's very interesting. Would it interest you to know that you have been followed for twenty-four hours? Would it further interest you to know that, at this point, as you sit in a drugstore on the corner of Columbus Avenue and Seventy-seventh Street, you are under the surveillance of what amounts almost to a small army of men? In fact, I would suggest you talk directly into the mouthpiece since someone may be able to read lips."

I decided, from the increased dryness of his voice, that the last suggestion was sarcasm. But I found myself wordless, nevertheless.

The silence stretched to a minute's worth before Mr. Roma spoke again. "But you pay us a compliment, Mr. Terrant. Although you have been unaware of my men, it has taken you only an hour to catch up with the strangers."

I chewed that over for a second. Then I began to swelter in the hot booth and sweat drained off me as, on a rising note, I said, "Then someone is—"

"Yes. You are leading a parade. After you come at least three strangers. After them come my men. And my men are increasing in number every minute, since you seem to be accomplishing something.

"I should be annoyed with you, Mr. Terrant. But I suppose your methods, which have a beautiful simplicity, may get results. So proceed, Mr. Terrant. We will do our best to protect you. My men have been extremely careful, and they're sure they have not been detected." The dry voice got a little warmer. "Two things, though: don't hope for too much. And—I wish you luck." He rang off.

And so I proceeded. As I worked my way along Seventy-seventh Street towards Central Park West my tenseness grew. I had a kind of lump in my throat. I found myself gulping insanely, as if for breath. And then I realized I was indeed gulping for breath; adrenalin was pouring into my heart from the increase of hope, fear, and desperation.

I listened with aching intensity to each formula answer. "What number did you want?" "What was that name?" "No, sorry. No Content here."

And finally, in the middle of the block, on the north side, it came. But it came unexpectedly. All my concentration on the nuances in the voices, all my studying of every face for the shades of reaction had been wasted effort.

I said to the tall, middle-aged, iron-grey woman who answered the door-bell, "Is Miss Ellen Content here?" and she said, "Yes. Come in."

I walked numbly across the dirty tiles of the vestibule, pushed the inner door wider, and, as the big woman moved back, I stepped into the dingy hallway. I don't think at that moment I believed her.

Somewhere in the back of my mind, which had almost stopped functioning, I thought she had misunderstood me, and that to my next question we would go back into the formula—"What was that name?" "No. Sorry"—but she wasn't put to the test. Something behind me, something that had been behind the door, came down on my head with a crashing blow.

I remember having one clear thought, I *have* found Ellen.

24

I WAS awakened by someone's saying "John, John, John." I was wallowing in the mud in a bloody little hole called Balleroy, just north of Saint Lô, and Jim Turner was calling me. But that couldn't be true because Jim Turner had been killed two days later in Saint Clair. Besides, I was lying on a lumpy cot, a bed of some sort. With my eyes still closed, I turned my head to the right, towards the sound of the voice, and as I moved, thunder echoed through my temples. I steadied my head on my right ear and breathed with studied evenness for a minute, and then I opened my eyes. And I had found Ellen.

She was sitting in a chair about ten feet from me. She had on what looked like an old-fashioned nightgown; it was white and had ruffles at the throat and wrists. The bangs were gone; her hair was parted in the centre and bound in braids around her head. She had always been slight; now she was a wraith. She had always been pale; now she was the colour of very white paper. Her skin seemed tissue thin; the paper colour was threaded with blue watermarks—her fine veins showing through.

But the eyes were the same; the eyes I had seen in my hotel room, the eyes I had never forgotten—dark, steady, clear, warm, and intelligent. The essence of Ellen.

She didn't get out of her chair, and then I saw that she was bound—*wired*—to the chair. Her wrists were held to its arms, and her ankles were crossed and wired to its right front leg. Then, without looking down, I knew I, too, was pinioned in some way around the ankles and arms.

Ellen said again, "John, John," and I've never seen such beauty as came through the small white face. Then she said, "Please don't talk until you feel better."

I couldn't talk. My vocal cords seemed to be paralysed. I deliberately relaxed, trying to get command of myself. I moved my eyes, taking in as much of the small room as my position would permit. The floor was bare. There was the bed I was lying on, the chair Ellen sat on, and a table opposite the door. On the table was a comb and brush and a *World Almanac* that said "1942" in swash letters on its spine. Light filtered through the single window, which had an old-fashioned shutter closed on the outside.

And that was all. There was nothing else in the room but Ellen.

Ellen had followed my eyes. She said, "I've been in this room since a few days after I last saw you. That *Almanac* saved me—my mind. I asked for a book. One of the crueller ones—he's gone now—gave me that. He thought it was a joke. Actually, for my kind of mind, it was the best possible diversion. Since then it has become a part of the room to them, and they no longer even see it—my salvation."

I was feeling a little better. In lieu of words, I managed a smile, and Ellen smiled back. Then she lifted a finger of her right hand and moved it in arcs—apparently to catch my attention. When my dulled eyes finally fastened on the finger, she started to point. She traced and retraced a line that went from the top of the window, along the moulding, and down the side of the door. With her lips she formed words without sound, and finally I understood.

"Dictaphone" . . . "locked in my bathroom" . . . "strapped so we . . . talk loud enough."

When she saw that I understood, she silently formed a question: "You aren't alone, John?"

"Whole army behind me," I breathed.

Thanksgiving glowed on her face like an answered prayer. She said, in the smallest of whispers, "They'll need time. I'll stall—talk— tell mostly truth. That will hold the interest of the people inside, keep them off."

Then she spoke aloud. "Are you hurt badly, John? Have they hurt you very much?"

I struggled, but no sound came.

"I'm sorry, darling. Rest for a while. I'll talk. I'll tell you about these people—these cruel, devious people, who are so strangely simple. Their simplicity has come to fascinate me. With no limit on the time I had to spend in watching and studying them, I've learned to follow their thought processes easily.

"First I tried to figure out why they didn't kill me. But that turned out to be an almost childishly simple problem—they simply weren't sure I hadn't passed the secret on. If I had, they needed me to guide them to its recapture. I told them and told them that no one else knew, but of course they never believed me—they're not *that* simple."

My fumbling mind worked over the words. But no one else *did* know. I spoke my first word—with a thick tongue, I produced a tender sound. "Ellen."

"Hush, darling." She shook her head in silent warning. "Rest for a while.

"Well, after I had figured that out I went on to the next logical question: if they thought someone else knew, why didn't they *extract* the information from me? Why was I unharmed?

"The answer to that one wasn't so easy to find. But simple logic finally gave it to me. They wanted me intact. And then it took me quite a while to guess why. They wanted me whole, so they must want to be able to produce me—*or my body!* That answered it. Our people were not, apparently, acting on my information."

Ellen flashed me a wan but impish smile. *Of course* the United States was not acting on the information—they didn't *have* it.

"From there on," she said, "it was pretty clear sailing. If, as the Russians suspected—and I did my best to make them think so—my knowledge was still available, possibly held by a person who did not realize its importance—then they had a use for me. As soon as they had a clue that the secret had reached the United States Government they would simply produce my body—floating down the Hudson, perhaps—neatly equipped with papers that proved me a Communist agent. It was really an ingenious plan. It would certainly serve to discredit the information—for a considerable amount of time, at least.

"Finally, when our Government showed no signs of knowledge after all this time, it was safe for them to make another move—the final effort to protect themselves against the possibility I constantly suggested and they dared not overlook: that the secret was not mine alone.

"Still holding me intact for future use, they would *trick* me into divulging whether or not my hints were true. They would give me what looked like a chance to get a message out. And they would be watching all the time, masters of the situation, ready to pounce.

"But then they made their usual mistake—they don't understand people and they underestimate people. I had learned to understand them, but they had never bothered to think of me as a person at all. I was merely a pawn. So when they set their trap, although it was devious, as usual, it was as transparent to me as their every move had come to be. They simply moved without giving me credit for any intelligence.

"A maid, a stolid, stupid, unfeeling woman, suddenly got sentimental and tender. She was being permitted to go home, she said, and if I wished, she'd carry a message out for me. On their part it was a rank, obvious gesture, but from my point of view it was a wonderful opportunity. After two years, I had a chance."

Ellen paused and looked around the barren room. "In almost two years, I've been out of this room only twice. I don't know what women are wearing or what happened to the United Nations. But I did manage to find out where I am.

"When they took me out the first time—to fix the ceiling—they put me in a front room. I got a glimpse of the street before they locked the shutters. I photographed that glimpse in my mind and pored over the mental picture for weeks until I finally placed it as Seventy-seventh between Columbus and the park. I was right, wasn't I?"

I nodded.

She said, "Yes. I used to live a little less than two blocks from here. I walked past this house every day on my way to the subway." She lapsed into silence.

I was feeling considerably better. I lifted my head, and after the blackness thinned away, noticed that my hands were not very securely tied. They hadn't bothered with wire for me; they had used some not-too-substantial rope. Whoever had delivered the rabbit punch apparently thought I'd be paralysed for hours.

I started working to loosen my hands. I looked at Ellen, nodded at the rope, and smiled. She smiled back encouragement. "Tell me about the maid," I said. My voice sounded rusty.

"Oh, yes. Well, she said she would be around for the last time in the morning, and I could give her this one message. So I had almost twelve hours in which to think it out.

"Believe me, John, it was the greatest problem of my life. They certainly weren't going to deliver an SOS to the CIA or to the local police precinct. They expected—hoped—I would send a message to the others who might know. In order to make them think I was doing just that it would be best if my message involved the original principals. That way, they would think they were getting somewhere, and I could hope they would be encouraged to go on with it. Then I thought of Natasha."

"Why not me?" I asked. My hands were almost free.

"How could I know if they knew about you? Besides, John, I've had a long time to think—and to remember that I saw you only four times—nineteen hours altogether. It would have been easy to—to take too much for granted."

"You couldn't have."

Ellen smiled. "But I couldn't be sure of that. Anyway, it would have put you in danger, and very possibly without accomplishing anything. By revealing Natasha's identity, I would seem to have been taken in. Of course, *she* would be in great danger, but—Well, I thought she would forgive me if I collected on a debt she swore she owed the last night I saw her. Especially since my release is really important to the—to the world."

My hands were free. I sat up and steadied myself against the wall. When the room stopped whirling and the sickness subsided, I started to loosen my feet.

Ellen nodded encouragingly and went on: "And then the message had to be mysterious, involved, devious. The Russian personality, which I now understand so well, would be captured by that. And it had to be confused enough so that although they wouldn't be able to solve it, our people would. In a way it was a test of our intelligence against theirs. I know the New York and London papers report sailings of passengers of interest. So part of the message was that Natasha's trip was to be a dancing engagement. If I had the luck to have it come to someone's attention—"

"But all you stipulated was that she dance in four towns?"

"Yes. And go to the St. Regis. In addition to trying to get across the idea of the 'street' I thought the Russians would be encouraged by the suggestion that a message might be there."

I made up my mind then and there that, if we got out of that room alive and free, Ellen was never to know of the death of Stephanie Stetson. At least—I amended it—not for a long time, not until she was strong.

There was no need for her to know; I was sure I could make Roma see that. And although Ellen was patently guiltless and too clear-minded to delude herself into an illusion of guilt, she was by the same token clear-minded enough to see and be made miserable by the other side of the coin: that she was an innocent accessory before the fact, and that her very innocence was the pivot on which Miss Stetson had turned from life to death.

I said, "Perhaps they were encouraged by the message, but they put their whole heart in the project from the very beginning. For instance, they went to a good deal of work to ensure the smooth carrying out of the trip by arranging bookings in advance in great detail."

"I was sure they would do that."

I was standing, very unsteadily. Ten feet from me was Ellen. I started weaving slowly towards her. As I got nearer, the little white face got smaller and whiter, and the big dark eyes seemed bigger and darker. When I reached her, I sank helplessly to my knees and buried my face in her lap.

We stayed that way for a minute, and then I raised my head and looked into Ellen's face. Tears were running down her cheeks, but she looked at peace, very much at peace.

Then she shook her head as if returning to the world and whispered to me. "Your army will be here any second. But—the first thing the people in the house will do is come for me, to come to—" She broke off.

I didn't think I could handle anyone. I could barely keep my head from rocking on my shoulders. Ellen saw it, and I think there was more compassion in her eyes for me than fear for herself.

I formed the word, "Talk!" and started unwinding the fine wire from around her ankles.

Ellen said clearly, pitching her voice to the bed across the room, "And after all, I've accomplished nothing. Now you are here, too, and they have both of us—" Her clear, sweet voice went on while I freed her. Then, while she talked on, I stood helplessly, with my arms around her, leaning a bit and trying to clear my mind.

My eyes went down to the coil of wire I had removed from Ellen's wrists and ankles. I couldn't fight anyone, but all we needed was time.

I motioned to Ellen to go on talking, and I moved across the room. I closed the bathroom door, which was at a right angle to the room's door, touching the same wall. On the bottom hinge, about a foot from the floor, I wound one end of the wire. Holding the remainder in my hand, I moved along the wall to the other side of the room's door. Then, leaving the wire slack, I wound the other end around my left ankle.

I stood still, bracing myself against the wall, and looked around, checking on the only articles the room contained—bed, chair, *Almanac,* comb, brush. None of them seemed very lethal. I reached out and pulled the chair towards me, and then discovered that I was unable to raise it to my shoulder. Ellen came and helped. After we had got it propped on my shoulder with my hands balancing the two front legs, Ellen squatted beside me and started to loosen the laces of the shoe of my unfettered foot. I didn't understand what she wanted it for, but I obediently lifted my foot out of the shoe.

Then Ellen arose and stood sturdily beside me, holding the big shoe, heel forward and downward, in her small hand. She had found another weapon in the room.

Ellen had given up any pretence of talking, and there we stood in silence, rather ridiculously, I suddenly thought—huddled against one wall of a shabby, empty room, holding our silly weapons. Ellen looked like a child in her long, shapeless gown, and I was weaving on my feet. I looked down at her around the chair and started to mention that we didn't seem very formidable, but at that moment she whispered up at me, "John, how are we doing in Korea?"

The effect of the question on me was devastating. I wasn't in command of myself yet, and it was such an odd, politically conscious, after-tea-party conversational gambit that hysteria threatened me. Laughter had begun to rumble in my throat when I suddenly went cold—like a drunk dumped into a cold bath.

"Ellen," I said, "how—"

And then we heard it. Into the quiet day, broken only by distant traffic sounds, came whistles, voices apparently thrown through megaphones, and a thunder of running feet.

The sounds were unplaceable, indefinable; they were all around us, beside us, under us and then one sound stood out. One set of running feet was coming upstairs, *towards* us.

I held to my chair, Ellen held to her shoe and, I realized, to my suit jacket.

The feet stopped at the door; there was a fumbling at the lock; and then the door was thrown—as I had hoped—violently open.

He came hurtling in, foolishly shooting as he entered. I raised my foot as he cleared the door, and he went over the wire and up into the air in a startling way, as if he were flying or swimming. His second, involuntary, bullet thudded into the *Almanac,* and then he landed flat on his stomach. I am certain that his forehead, belt buckle, and toes all touched ground at once—and as he hit the ground I brought, the chair down on the back of his head.

Unfortunately, the chair didn't behave according to the best traditions of all rough and tumble. It seemed to me that it was supposed to break into pieces, thus supplying me with a handy truncheon. Nothing, I thought grimly—as I straddled the figure and slowly, laboriously, but repeatedly lifted the heavy chair and brought it down on the head beneath me—nothing behaved according to plan during the Content assignment.

Behind me I became aware that Ellen, too, was straddling the man and bludgeoning him with my shoe. It came to me, through my concentration, that she must be attacking his buttocks, and that seemed rather profitless. I was gathering breath to explain that to her when a soft, very calm voice spoke from the rear of us.

"Miss Content. Mr. Terrant. I really think the gentleman is unconscious."

We stopped in slow motion. I turned—it was an effort—and found that Mr. Kennedy was standing in the hall surveying us through the open doorway. He was smiling, and there seemed to be a group of men behind him. I put my arm around Ellen and tried to lift the two of us off the prone figure beneath us, and then I found that I couldn't get my knees under me.

The smile left Kennedy's face, and then it seemed to me that Kennedy's face left, too.

It became most confused.

At some juncture I found myself standing on the pavement, although I knew I hadn't been standing before. Ellen was in front of me. She had on a brown mackintosh. She looked just as she had in the hotel lobby in Berlin, and I wondered if she'd lost her blue scarf. And then I realized it was much too warm for the mackintosh. I started to say so when I noticed that Mr. Roma was standing beside her. It struck me that he was an anachronism, and then I discovered the odd fact that my head was revolving in a three hundred and sixty degree circle, and Mr. Roma kept sailing past.

Someone caught me by the elbow.

Mr. Roma said, "We're going to borrow Miss Content for twenty-four hours or so, Mr. Terrant. Just for a flying trip to Washington and back. Meanwhile you'll go to your hotel—"

"I know," I said. "I'm to go to my hotel and wait there. I'm just to stay there and wait. I'm not to—"

But Mr. Roma had the last word. "For goodness' sake, take him to his hotel and put him to bed," he said.

25

It wasn't twenty-four hours; it was nearly forty-eight hours before Ellen returned. But the hours went quickly because I was unconscious for most of them. The doctor, who in his dryness reminded me of Roma, merely said I was "out on my feet" and then ensured that fact by stuffing me full of sedatives.

But when she came it was as if she had never been away. The forty-eight hours were forgotten; the two years were gone. She was escorted into my room by Roma, who muttered something about being right back and faded out of the door. I don't think I said hello to him.

Ellen sat on a chair near the door, and again—I from a bed and she from a chair—we looked at each other. She had a blue scarf around her neck, and it was as if time had never passed. She still looked white and very, very frail, but she was beautiful as no other woman in the world is beautiful.

I said, "And now it'll be all right for us."

"For us?" she asked, and then, with a nod, "For us."

We were silent for a minute. Then she said, "One thing. Will you be able to bear not knowing most of the details? Because some of it I can never tell you."

I brushed that aside with a wave of my hand. "What has that to do with us? Except—" The question that had been occurring and recurring during my sleep-laden two days came back. "Except for one thing. You asked about Korea. How did you know about Korea?"

Ellen sighed. "All those years of self-control, even despite—persuasion, and then seeing you—unsettled me. I just couldn't wait to know—I suppose, then, I'll have to explain the basic fact. The secret, you see, the thing I knew."

I nodded.

"Well, I had the Russian timetable—the details, the plans, the strategy, for years and years to come."

The enormity of it caught at me for a minute. But that was all I'd ever know about it, and my personal life was for that moment in eternity, much larger. I said, "Ellen, please come here."

And she came towards me.